Diary
of a
SUPER GIRL

Book 1

The Ups and Downs
of
Being Super

John Zakour & Katrina Kahler

Table of Contents

The Long Day...

"I leaped across the parking lot towards this black van car. The bad guys were in it. They turned and saw me and hit the gas! I leaped again and picked up the car like it weighed nothing! I turned the car over and shook it until the bad guys fell out...They rolled to the ground and then each ran off in opposite directions...I took off my shoe and tossed it at one of them. It hit him on the back of the head...he fell to the ground, out cold. Truthfully, I'm not sure if he was knocked out by the force or the smell of the shoe!

I turned to see the other guy. No way was I letting him get

away!"

I noticed my hands had clenched into fists as I told my story to Jason.

"Then what happened?" Jason asked me, a smile on his face.

"Then I woke up...," I said.

"Bummer," he said, his smile fading. "It sounded like a great dream, Lia!"

"It seemed so real!" I said with a shrug. "I blame you! You're the one always talking about super heroes and comic books!"

"Well, comics are awesome," he said.

It had been a LONG day at school. Still, no matter how terrible my school day went I always enjoyed my walk home with my best friend, Jason. Okay, I know what you're thinking, he's a boy and he's a friend, but he's not my boyfriend. We're more like BFFs. Mom and I moved to our new home in Starlight City when I was three. I walked out of my house and saw three-year-old Jason playing with Lego in his yard, alongside his mom. My mom and I walked over. Jason handed me a piece of Lego and said, "Play!" I smiled and said, "Yes!" Hey, we were three years old. We didn't have the biggest vocabulary back then. But we still knew, at first sight, we'd be friends forever.

Yeah, it's kind of funny to be BFF with a boy but since that day we have shared everything. Maybe someday it could turn into more of a crush. After all, I guess he's good looking and all and he's really fun to hang out with. But like I said, I've known him forever, well at least as long as I can remember. So, dating him might be weird. In many ways, we're like brother and sister, except of course we get along really well.

"So. How'd you do on the science test?" Jason asked, coaxing me to the present.

"I can't believe I got a B on that," I sighed in frustration. "I thought for sure I had an A- at worst. I studied the planets in our system so well. I remembered all the moons. I knew Pluto is now a dwarf planet…Which I don't agree with BTW." I looked at Jason in disgust. I should definitely have got at least an A-.

He smiled sympathetically. "I'm with you on that. I mean come on, how can Pluto be a planet one day and some other day it's not. Just because a bunch of space research people said it's not big enough to be a planet?" He paused for a second. "Oh, when I say it like that, I can kind of see why they changed their mind…I guess I'm just not big on change."

"Me either," I replied.

Then something else came to mind that I was also annoyed about. "And it's not fair that lacrosse practice is so hard. I swear coach Blue thinks we're training for the Olympics or something. She ran us up and down the field so many times. I believe my sweat was breaking out in sweat. I desperately need a shower. I must really smell right now…"

"I haven't noticed," Jason said politely. He pointed to his nose and smiled. "Of course, I do have a head cold."

I gave him a friendly little shove. He playfully went staggering backward like I had pushed him too hard. "Be careful!" he said, fake rubbing his arm. "You are way strong!"

I shook my head, "Not according to our team captain, Miss Perfect, Wendi Long. She said that I need to work on my abs and my wrist shot… I'm surprised she didn't critique my breath and hair style…"

Jason shrugged. "Ah, you can't blame Wendi. She's not a bad person, it's just that being perfect comes naturally to her."

I gave him another friendly little push. "You just say that because she's the best-looking girl in the school…"

"Well yeah, but only if you like golden blond hair, sea blue eyes, and perfectly clear peach complexion…." He grinned.

I sighed. "Yeah, she seems immune to zits…Unlike me. I have one on my nose that needs its own postal code."

Jason laughed. "It's not that bad. Nobody has called you Rudolph yet…" He paused for a second. "You ready f or the big day tomorrow?"

"You mean the math quiz?" I said though I knew what he was getting at.

"No, you turn the big 1-3 tomorrow. You become a teen!"

"Well, *you* became a teen last week," I said. "So far, have you seen any difference between being a teen and a tween?"

Jason stopped walking. He looked up at the clear blue sky and thought for a moment. Scratching his head, he said, "Now that you mention it, I feel older. I think my back cracks more and I believe I might have a gray hair…"

"Ha ha!" I told him.

He gave me a friendly pat on the shoulder. "Nah, so

far 12 and 13 seem the same to me. But who knows, maybe for you, it will be different. After all, girls mature quicker than boys…" he said.

I laughed. "We do mature mentally faster!"

Jason started using his fist to make noises with his arm pit. "What makes you say that?" he said squeaking away.

We laughed all the way to our houses.

Home Sweet Home...

I got home and kicked my shoes off the second I walked in the door. Shep, my ever-loyal German Shepherd ran up to me, tail wagging away. It's great to come home to somebody who is so excited to see me. Shep licked me a few times as I bent over to pat him. Then he turned his attention to my shoes. For some reason, he always insists on sniffing my shoes when I get home.

"Ah, Shep those things probably smell really bad!" I warned. "It's been a long day."

But that didn't stop Shep. He sniffed my shoes contentedly. "Wow, you are a tough dog!" I laughed.

Walking into the living room, I plopped down on the couch. I needed a nap. Funny thing was when I was a little kid I HATED naps. I guess I felt that I'd miss out on something if I slept. Today, after a day of tests and practice I needed a 20-minute power nap. It wasn't just the work that got to me. Sometimes I felt the hardest part of middle school was dealing with other middle school kids who I couldn't help thinking were always rating me and comparing me to other girls. There were so many things to worry about. Right then, I had a giant zit on my nose and was sure that everyone must have noticed it. But my main worry was what Wendi Long was saying about me on Facebook, as well as in private to her friends. I could only imagine what she said behind my back. Eventually, I fell asleep and dreamed of being an ugly duckling who turned into a beautiful swan. Weird!

I woke up a little later at the sound of the front door closing.

"Mom?" I called, half-awake from the couch. I pulled out my phone and looked at the time: 4:20, that was early for mom. "Is everything okay?"

She didn't usually leave work early. At least not since I was old enough to watch out for myself. Mom and I have been alone for as long as I can remember. In fact, I can barely recall my dad. But that's okay, Mom and I make a great team.

She walked into the living room still in her white medical scrubs. "I came home early," she said, looking at me curiously as I lay sprawled on the couch. "Looks and smells like you had a long day." She broke into a wide grin.

"Yeah, it's been pretty big," I replied. "I'm wrecked! What are we doing for dinner?"

"How's pizza sound?" she smiled.

"Like you read my mind!" I told her, my own face breaking into a smile of its own. "But you still haven't said why you're home early?"

"My last surgery got canceled so I figured I'd head home before they asked me to do something else…" She patted me on the legs. "Spend the evening with my daughter. After all, you're going to be 13 tomorrow…"

"I realize that, Mom."

She looked me in the eyes. "There's something I want to talk to you about, before the big day. Prepare you…."

My eyes popped open. "Mom! I know about the *birds and the bees* as you call it. You've already talked about that and then they talked about it at school as well."

She laughed. "No, it's not that. It's just well, your name is Lia Strong and you're part of the Strong family. You're also one of the Strong women. You don't know this yet, but all of us Strong women change when we hit the teen years," she was talking slowly, hoping I would understand.

"Mom, I know about puberty and the changes it brings!" I told her. I pointed to my body. "Some of them have started already!"

"That's actually not what I'm referring to." She stood up from the couch then bent down to touch her toes and stretched upwards again. "Strong women change, differently…."

"Mom, what are you talking about?"

Without another word, she bent down and picked up the couch with me on it. Then she lifted it over her head with one hand. And when I say lift it, she did it easily, like it was a twig.

"What the…."

"Lia! Watch your language!" she scolded before I could finish.

11

"Yeah, this is definitely different!" I said.

"I told you," Mom replied, lowering the couch with me still on it, back to the floor. "You take a shower and change while I order the food. We'll talk over pizza and wings."

"You drop this on me and then say, we'll chat in a bit?" I looked at her in amazement and shook my head. This was too much to take in.

She put a gentle hand on my shoulder. "Believe me, honey, this is a wonderful change. But like all changes, it will take some getting used to. But I promise you'll understand it better with a full stomach."

I sat up on the couch. "There were a lot of buts in that statement," I told her.

She smiled, and I could see she was not going to say another word. Finding it hard to believe what had just happened, I got up and headed upstairs. Right then, I figured it best not to argue with a mom who could lift the couch. If what she said was true, tomorrow I would be able to do that too. I had a million questions running through my brain. But Mom was right. This would all go down better after a shower and pizza. Not sure why, but a good shower always cleared my head. And tasty pizza puts me in a good mood. Yeah! My mom was one sharp lady.

The New Rules...

Mom and I sat down at the kitchen table, pizza and wings between us. Something about the smell of a pizza puts me at ease.

"So how was your day?" Mom asked pouring some pepper on her pizza.

"Mom! I'm been very patient so far!" I replied abruptly. Right then, I think I had the right to be frustrated.

She grinned. "Okay, okay...well...first off, being super is...well... super. We can do things other people only dream of..."

I nibbled on a piece of pizza and shook my head in agreement. "Yes, I noticed you lifting a couch like nothing... How strong are we?"

"Each of us differs. You know your grandma can still whip a gator like nothing. Your great grandma can lift over 300 pounds with one hand. Though of course she never does that in public. And she insists her mom could throw a tank the length of a football field easily..." Mom told me all of this in her most serious voice.

"Wow!" It was the only word I could think of as a response.

"Well put," Mom said munching on a wing. "We have other abilities too.... I'll only mention the basic ones until we see what ones show up in you. All our senses are very heightened. Our skin is very dense. Yes, it can be poked and penetrated by some sharp objects but we heal very quickly."

"So, we're like Wolverine in the X-men movies..."

Mom bobbed her head. "Kind of. Only no claws..."

"Phew!" I said.

"Oh, we also have super breath…" Mom told me, apparently reminded by my sigh. "Well, technically it's not the breath. Our lungs are just super powerful. Which means we can blow people away and toss them over and over."

I smiled. "Oh, that's so cool!"

"Except if you forget, and sneeze," she told me. "That can be bad!"

I slumped back in my chair.

"You just have to be calm and relax, Lia, and you'll be fine," She spoke with a confident assurance. But it was one that I certainly didn't feel. "Mom! I'm a teenage girl! Do you remember how hard that is??"

She laughed. "Yes, I remember the days. But when you're feeling stressed, close your eyes…take a few deep gentle breaths…ease them in and ease them out. All the while, imagine you're somewhere nice and quiet…by a pond or on a cloud….then count down from ten, slowly."

I did as she said. I closed my eyes, took a few breaths and then slowly counted backward from ten. I opened my eyes. I had to admit I felt calmer already. "Wow! That works!"

She pointed to the side of her head. "Med school, baby!"

Munching on another slice of pizza, she looked at me for a moment and then continued. "When touching, or grabbing objects or people, treat them like they are very fragile crystal…because to us they are…"

"You're kidding?" I asked, my eyebrows raised in disbelief.

She picked up a thick ceramic mug that she liked to drink coffee out of. It had to be the biggest, thickest mug in the house. I watched as she closed her hand around it. The mug crumpled into ceramic dust. My mouth dropped open.

"Lia, close your mouth," she shook her head at my wide-eyed expression. "Nobody wants to see what you're chewing…or, in this case, forgetting to chew."

"Oh wow!!" My mouth was still open, I was in total shock. When I saw her frown, I closed my mouth and did as I was told. Then I thought of an important question. "Does this mean I'll never be able to hold hands with my boyfriend?"

She shook her head. "No, of course not…"

"What do you mean?" I asked, a deep frown creasing my forehead. "No, of course, I won't be able to hold hands, or…no, of course, I will be able to hold hands?"

"Yes, Lia, with practice you'll be able to hold hands. It's not that bad. You just need to be aware of your strength." Mom smiled.

"Phew!"

"One thing, though," she nervously tapped the table. "Hygiene is super-duper important."

"Mom, I'm a girl in middle school, for us, hygiene is always important."

She nodded. "True. But now you're going to have to be extra cautious. I'll give you some of my super deodorant. That is the only type that will work."

A big smile crossed her face. "I actually developed it myself. It's good to know chemistry and the super human body so well. When I give it to you, make sure you use it on your underarms really well. You don't want to lift your arm up to ask a question and knock out half the class!"

I rolled my eyes. "Mom, I know how to use deodorant…"

"And your feet!" she cut me off urgently. "That's something you must not forget. You must coat them really well. And make sure you wear shoes that let your feet breathe. And of course, never ever, ever wear socks two days in a row. You want people to be able to keep breathing after you take your shoes off!"

"Mom! My feet don't smell! At least not THAT bad! Well, they're not lethal." I added, after a moment's thought.

"That's cause you're not super yet. Once it hits, look out. What you now think isn't that bad, will suddenly be able to drop a pack of charging rhinos from 30 feet away! You will definitely need my super deodorant!"

"Ah, okay," I replied, though I couldn't really believe that.

"Oh, and the reason why we never get pizza with onions and garlic is that it's very important for us never to eat anything that can give us gas." She stopped for a minute so I could consider what she'd said. "For some reason, our bodies are immune to certain things, but others we tend to make worse.... life's a tradeoff I guess."

"In other words, no bean burritos," I said jokingly.

She nodded firmly, her eyes locked on mine. "Definitely not. I had one at the zoo once by accident...the smell dropped the entire lion exhibition. It was empowering and embarrassing at the same time. If you ever do need to fart..."

"Mom, I never fart!"

She looked at me. "If you do need to fart, make sure you do it in a wide open well-aired place. Legend has it that one of our ancestors farted at the Gobi forest."

"Mom, the Gobi is a desert," I said very matter of fact.

Mom nodded. "It is now!" she replied straight-faced. "Plus, in 1908 your great, great, great, great, great Grandma Carol farted while camping in Siberia. The damage was so bad, scientists believe the place was devastated by an asteroid!"

"Anything else I should be aware of?" I asked fighting back a gulp.

"Sneezing!" Mom said. "Luckily being super, we are immune to most illnesses, but pepper and some foods can still make us sneeze. Just always cover your mouth if it happens. You don't want to sneeze down a building."

I nodded. "I can see why that would be bad."

"Yeah, great grandma once sneezed over a mountain...."

"Yikes!" I said. "These powers are kind of cool and scary at the same time!"

Mom leaned over and hugged me. "Yes, they are. Like I said, being super is wonderful, but at the same time, you have to be cautious. Life always comes with tradeoffs. Plus you have to keep the power a secret."

I leaned back in my chair and laughed. "Yeah, I guess we don't want to end up part of a secret government program!"

Mom hugged me again, she really liked to hug. "Not just that, but if people found out we could do super things they'd either be scared of us or want us to do special favors for them."

"Never thought of that," I said.

She grinned. "That's why I'm the mom!"

"So, when will this hit me?" I asked curiously.

Mom looked at her watch. "Well, you were born at 5 a.m. So anytime after that. It's not an exact science. Heck, I'm not even sure if it is a science. What I do know is that it's an amazing gift!"

"Well, this explains the dreams I've been having…about me lifting cars and battling bad guys. I blamed Jason's comics."

Mom patted me gently on the shoulder. "Nope, that's your subconscious kicking in and preparing you for what's to come!"

"Lovely," I said.

Mom looked me in the eyes. "Honey, this will be wonderful, tricky but wonderful. At times, it might be challenging, but challenges are good!" She kissed me on the forehead. "You'll be great!"

"I hope you're right!"

After dinner, I headed up to my room. To take my mind off my "problems" I did my homework. Of course, my English just happened to be reading, The Lion, The Witch and The Wardrobe. A story about kids learning how to deal with a strange world and their powers in that world. Kind of ironic I guess. I went to bed that night half thrilled, half worried. I wasn't sure if I would still be me when I woke up. Mom had to be exaggerating the problems of being super. She HAD to be.

After a while, I fell asleep. First of all, I dreamed of leaping through the air and then the dream became a nightmare when I crashed down in the middle of the city, causing a huge crater. I looked at the crater and said, "Oops, my bad…."

Morning comes...

The next thing I knew I felt something wet on my face, desperately trying to wake me up. I forced my eyes to pop open. There stood Shep licking me. I took a second to collect myself. I still felt like me. Maybe my powers hadn't kicked in yet? Maybe Mom was wrong about me? Shep persisted in licking me, hoping I would get up.

I laughed and said, "Shep *stop!*"

Suddenly he did stop. And when I say stop, I mean he went stiff and fell to the ground with a clunk.

"MOM!" I shouted.

Mom leaped up the stairs, she was in my doorway in less than a second.

"MOM! LOOK WHAT I DID TO POOR SHEP! MOM! WHAT DID I *DO* TO POOR SHEP?"

Mom staggered back a step and covered her nose. "Super morning bad breath!" she said, shaking her head and bending down to check on our poor dog.

I stuck my hand over my nose and lips and puffed a little breath into my hand. I crinkled my nose. "Sure my breath is a kind of bad, but not bad enough to drop a 120-pound guard dog in his tracks...."

"Not to you or I, because we're super, but to non-supers," she nodded to Shep with her head, "It's a different story."

I sat up in bed. "Is he dead?" I gasped.

Mom shook her head. She gave Shep a few rapid pats to his chest and he sprang back to life. I breathed a huge sigh of relief. My breath hit Shep and he passed out again. Mom rolled her eyes. "Honey, you have to be careful!" she started patting his chest once more.

"Right!" I said covering my mouth. "Oh no! Does this mean I'll never be able to kiss my husband good morning without killing him?"

Mom smiled. "You'll learn to control it, especially by the time you get married…many, many years from now."

I could only hope Mom was right about this.

She picked Shep up like he was a little puppy then motioned to the bathroom with her head. "Now go wash up. And don't forget your super deodorant. We'll go over the dos and don'ts again during breakfast."

"Right," I said. I got up and walked to my bathroom door. I grabbed the door knob and pulled the door off the hinges like it weighed nothing. Yep, this would take some getting used to. "Ah Mom, maybe I should take a sick day today!"

Mom smiled and shook her head. "Nonsense. The best way for you to learn to control your powers is to be out in the world."

"It will force you to concentrate on being careful." She walked out of the room but called over her shoulder. "I'm making your favorite for breakfast, pancakes with blueberries."

I could only hope Mom was right. After all Middle School came with enough problems already, without me having to worry about farts that actually really were silent but deadly.

Breakfast Time...

I hurried into my now doorless bathroom ready to hit the showers. First, though, I stopped and looked in the mirror over the sink. Yep, I still looked like me, brown hair, blue eyes...a nose that had a zit on it. But then I noticed the zit was gone. Okay, so I guess something good had come from being super.

I got in the shower and scrubbed and cleaned like I had never done before. Oh, don't get me wrong, I take my showering very seriously. If you're a girl in middle school and you smell, you are marked for life. But today I made extra certain I didn't miss a spot.

After the shower, I used generous portions of mom's super deodorant on any part of me that might sweat. I tossed on my school uniform. It's a perfect drab white shirt with brown shorts. In a way, I like having a school uniform. It cuts down some of the drama of what to wear each school day. Of course, we still get to accessorize though. Today I decided to go with a nice pendant my great, great grandma had given me.

By then, the smell of pancakes had worked its way up to my room. That smell called me down to breakfast.

I felt relieved to see that Mom really had prepared my favorite breakfast of blueberry pancakes, wheat toast with fruit and a glass of fresh orange juice. I needed something normal to start this far from normal day.

As I ate, Mom lectured.

"Okay, controlling your strength is easy as pie."

"Is that a medical term, Mom?"

"Ha ha! Just when squeezing or grabbing a person or thing, take a deep breath and mentally think they are made of fine crystal."

"Got it, breathe and take it easy," I said.

"Foods to avoid: onions, garlic, beans, anything that could give you bad breath or gas."

"Luckily, I'm a girl in middle school so I normally avoid those anyhow."

"You used my special deodorant, right?" Mom asked, proudly.

"Yep!"

"You packed it in your school bag just in case, right?"

"Yes. Mom."

She leaned over and gave me a kiss. "Well, I think you're ready for the world!"

"Let's just hope the world is ready for me!" I sighed.

With that, I heard a knock at the door. "Wait, is that Jason?"

Mom sniffed the air. "Yes, I can smell his brand of hair gel from here," Mom pointed to her nose. "Super sense of smell," she smiled.

I sniffed the air. Now that Mom mentioned it, I could smell it too. "Wow, I had no idea that stuff had such a strong scent," I pulled out my phone and looked at the time. I had to get moving.

Leaping up, I grabbed my book bag, took one last sip of juice and gave Mom a kiss goodbye.

"Are you sure I'm ready for this?"

She put both her hands on my shoulders and looked me in the eyes. "Lia, nobody is ever ready for this. But you are as ready as you can be. When you get out there in the world with your friends you will learn and adapt." She smiled. "I'm sure of it!" Kissing me on the forehead, she waved me out of the kitchen.

I took a deep breath and turned towards the door.

Same Walk, Different Me...

Jason rang the doorbell again. My phone buzzed. It was a text from him.

JASON> I'm here! ☺

LIA> Yep, figured it out :-) Coming!

JASON> OK

Funny how HE seemed extra anxious today. I opened the door and there stood Jason, a smile on his dimpled cheeks and holding a blueberry muffin with a candle on it.

"Happy Birthday!" he shouted, handing me the muffin. "Blow out the candle!" he coaxed.

Okay, now this could be tricky. I took the muffin and turned it away from him, just in case I hit it with too much power. I puffed my lips and concentrated on letting out just a little whiff of air. My breath hit the candle, the candle fizzled out and then fell to the ground. I guess it could have been worse.

"Wow, I see you're extra pumped today!" Jason said, giving me a hug.

I hugged him back, concentrating on being gentle. He didn't yelp in pain so I think I succeeded. "Thanks!" I said, smiling at him. The muffin and candle had been such a sweet thing to do.

I bent down and picked up the candle.

"Now that you're a full teen do you feel different?" Jason asked.

I nodded and smiled. "You'd be surprised!"

My walk to school with Jason was always the calm before the storm of the day. I liked the fact that we still walked. It gave us time to talk and it dragged out the start of each day at school.

"Read any good comic books lately?" I asked.

Jason's face lit up. "What really? Do you really want to know? Usually when I talk about comic books your face goes kind of blank. I know you're trying to be polite, but comics and super heroes aren't your favorite things. You always say, I like to stay grounded in what's *real*," he said that last part badly imitating my voice.

"Wow that was horrible," I said, giving him a little shove.

He went flying much farther to the side than I had intended. He staggered to a stop and said, "Impressive!"

"I've been working out. Remember that captain Wendi Long said I need to pump up," I told him. "Now, how about those comics?"

His face lit up. "I've been rereading the Death of Superman!" he said, almost popping out of his socks with excitement.

"Wait. Superman dies??"

Jason nodded. "Yeah, he sacrifices himself to save Earth from an evil clone of himself...the comic is kind of like the movie but better." Jason must have noticed the look of concern on my face. "But Superman does come back."

"Phew," I said, though really, I had no idea why that made me feel better.

Suddenly we heard a loud angry barking. The barking got louder and louder. Both Jason and I knew who the culprit was. We turned to see, Cuddles, the meanest nastiest Doberman pincher on Earth running towards us, fangs out. Cuddles' owner, a sweet old blue haired lady named Ms. Jewel, ran after him, desperately trying to stop him.

"Cuddles! Stop! Stop!" she ordered.

Cuddles continued to race towards us and the open gate to his lawn.

"Sorry kids! He got away from me again!" Ms. Jewel

called puffing after her dog.

Jason and I both froze in our places. We had been through this drill before. Cuddles would approach us. Sniff us. Growl at us. And then decide we were no threat as long as we stayed off of his yard. And you can bet that was our plan.

This time though, when Cuddles got within sniffing range, he jammed to a sudden stop. He looked me in the eyes. He rolled over and whimpered.

"Now, that's different!" Jason said.

"I guess he knows we're mostly harmless," I replied, giving myself a quick whiff of my underarms to make sure I still smelled fresh. Thankfully, I did.

Jason shrugged. We continued on our way to school. I pulled out my phone and sent a fast text to my mom.

LIA> OK, that was weird. Cuddles the world's worst named dog stopped charging and rolled over when he got a whiff of me and I don't smell bad at all!

MOM> That's because animals can sense our power

LIA> Good 2 no

MOM> Honey I know this is a txt but still use the right words please!

LIA> Good 2 know

MOM> Thk u! ☺

Locker Talk...

Jason and I stood at our lockers pulling out the books we'd need for first and second period while putting away the stuff we wouldn't need. I like morning locker time, it gives me a chance to catch up on what's going on. I even kind of liked the bright green barf color of the halls. Something about them mixed with the orange lockers made the school look like it had been designed by a colorblind clown. Somehow it was a look that clicked with my tastes.

One of my friends, Krista Johnson, raced across the hallway towards me. Krista is very pretty, with long wavy blond hair and huge blue eyes. She's just...how can I say this politely? Forgetful. As usual, I was sure she needed something from me.

"Hey! Lia! Happy, happy, happy BIRTHDAY!" she squealed, bubbling with excitement. She hugged me. I hugged her back as gently as I could. She didn't scream. I took that as another good sign. I was really catching on to this super strength stuff.

But then she frowned and sniffed the air.

You smell different!

"You smell different," she said, a curious expression on her face.

"Ah, new deodorant," I replied slowly.

Krista smiled. "Wow, it's a nice one!"

"Thanks," I replied, relieved. I only hoped it kept working as the day dragged on.

Krista stood there looking at me, tapping her foot.

"Do you need something, Krista?" Jason asked. Jason wasn't as patient as I am with her.

"Not from you silly, but from Lia!" Krista looked at me. It kind of reminded me of how a doe looks when it's confused. "Ah, we have lacrosse practice today. Right?"

I nodded. "It's a week day so yes, yes we do," I told her.

Krista put her arms behind her back and started wobbling back and forth. "Ah, do you like possibly maybe have an extra stick for me to use...I left mine at home. I could run home after practice but then I'll be late and Wendi will yell at me. I don't want that!"

I turned to my locker. Luckily I always kept an extra lacrosse stick in there, just in case. I pulled out the stick and handed it to Krista.

"Is that a yes?" Krista asked me.

"Yes!" Jason and I both answered together.

Krista took the stick and hugged me again. Of course, she poked Jason and me with the stick. Jason staggered back a step. I didn't even feel it. "Thank you! Thank you! Thank you!" she said. "I'll return it once I remember to bring mine!"

Krista walked away humming.

"You might not ever see that stick again," Jason said.

Tim Dobbs a short, stocky kid with a brush cut rushed up to his locker. Tim almost always had on headphones and was always running late. Still, he was a good guy. "Hey, Lia, Happy Birthday!" he told me, actually taking his headphones off.

"Thanks, Tim!" I said.

Tim gave Jason a nod. "Hey!"

"Hey!" Jason responded.

When it comes to male communication I swear boys aren't much more advanced than cavemen.

"Wow, everybody knows it's your b-day," Jason said nudging me. "You must be famous."

"Nah, but I do have Facebook!"

From behind me, I heard. "Oh, Lia!"

I knew that perfect lyrical voice. It belonged to our lacrosse captain and home coming queen, Wendi Long. I turned and saw Wendi strutting towards me. She had long blond hair that seemed to dance on her shoulders, bright blue eyes, a perfect nose, perfect teeth and the most beautiful skin that I was sure had never seen a zit. Seeing such perfection walk towards me, I sighed.

My sigh drove her back a few steps. I'd have to be careful with that. I'd also have to be careful that I enjoyed doing that.

"What's up, Wendi?" I asked.

The second that Wendi reached us, I swear Jason's IQ was cut in half. "Ah... ah....hi...Wendi..." he stuttered.

Wendi stood there, arms crossed looking me in the eyes. "Remember we're starting practice at 2:45 today!" she announced.

"Yes, like we do every day!" I answered.

"I just wanted to make sure you're on time today. We're scrimmaging and you'll be leading the squad that's playing against my squad. I want to make sure you are at your best to give us as much of a test as possible." Wendi's mouth was a firm line. She took her job as team captain very seriously.

I nodded. "Don't worry, I look forward to playing against you."

Looking over Wendi's shoulder, I spotted Brandon Gold coming towards us. Brandon is captain of all the sports teams, class president and top student in the class. Plus, if he wanted to be, he could be a male model as well, as he was so good looking. His only flaw was that he went out with Wendi.

"Hey, Lia! Happy Birthday!" Brandon smiled. I swear his teeth glistened.

"Ah, thanks," I said as calmly as possible. While my insides were saying "HOLY COW!!! BRANDON KNOWS WHO I AM!! HE KNOWS IT'S MY BIRTHDAY! HE SPOKE TO ME!"

"Hey, how do you know it's her birthday?" Wendi demanded.

"It's on Facebook!" Brandon told her.

"And you're friends with Lia?" Wendi asked as if she were talking about the king greeting a peasant.

"Yeah," Brandon answered simply as if it was no big deal.

Wendi pulled Brandon away. "Come on, we'll be late for class!" she frowned at him and grabbed his arm.

"Bye guys!" Brandon waved as Wendi dragged him down the hall.

"What does a guy like Brandon see in Wendi anyhow?" I asked, louder than I intended to.

"Maybe because she's so good looking," Jason replied.

"Oh, plus she's rich!" he added.

"Okay, I get the point. I just think Brandon can do better."

Jason grinned. "You may be a bit biased. After all, you and Wendi have been rivals for a while now."

I shook my head. "Not sure how we're rivals, she wins all the time."

Jason patted me on the shoulder. "Nah, you're being too hard on yourself." He stopped talking. "Oh no, speaking of rivals, here comes Tony Wall."

I turned to see Tony walking steadily towards us. Tony had just finished "borrowing" lunch money from some younger kids. Now he had his sights set on Jason. Tony was a classic bully, he wasn't very smart but when you're bigger than everybody else, there's not a lot of need for brains. I might have had to deal with Wendi but no way was I going to let Tony bully my best friend. We only had a minute until the morning bell so I just needed to delay him.

I inhaled and then softly exhaled in Tony's direction. He went staggering back and hit the lockers behind him. A couple of the smaller kids also blew backward but they were too amused by Tony smacking into the lockers to really care. A bunch of kids (including the smaller ones) began to laugh.

"Quit laughing!" Tony ordered, fists curled.

"Hey, Tony? What happened?" Brandon called to him. Brandon happened to be one of the few kids in the school Tony didn't try to bully.

Tony shook his head. "I don't know…some sort of crazy draft in the school today."

"I felt it too!" Wendi said.

I had to confess a part of me enjoyed using super breath on Tony. Yeah, I pushed back a few innocent kids too, but it was all for the greater good. Now I knew Mom wasn't joking when she said no onions or garlic. That could have been dangerous. Well, fun for me but dangerous for everybody else. I didn't need that. Right? I had to use this power for good. I mean that had to be the reason I had this power? To help the world? Of course, there's nothing wrong with having fun too. Is there? Before I could think too long, the morning bell rang. I snapped back to reality. Of course, my reality was different now. It was going to be challenging on all sorts of levels, but I knew I could handle it.

I had to!

Class Time...

My morning classes were three of my most challenging: Science, Math, and English. But the good news is, I really enjoy a challenge. The bad news is, Mr. Ohm our Science (and Math due to budget cuts) teacher was handing back our science quizzes from yesterday. Mr. Ohm handed me my test. I like Mr. Ohm I believe he's a good guy. Sometimes, since he's single and decent looking (for a teacher), I think he could be a good match for my mom.

Other times, I think having a teacher around all the time would not be good at all. Mr. Ohm looked directly at me when he gave me my paper. It had a score of 85 on it.

"Not bad," he told me. "It was a hard quiz…"

"I didn't think it was THAT hard," Wendi said.

"Oh man, I thought it was way hard!" Krista added.

I knew from the tone of his voice Mr. Ohm was disappointed in me. But not nearly as disappointed as I was in myself. I had studied so hard. But when I glanced through the test I saw where I'd gone wrong. Somehow, I thought Pan and Narvi were moons of Jupiter, and there was a Saturn moon. I was so annoyed with myself for getting those three wrong.

Mr. O must have noticed the look of disappointment on my face. "Cheer up!" he encouraged. "You can do a paper for extra credit if you want." He looked up at the class. "You all can if you wish."

Some of the kids sighed in relief, others groaned, others sat there still trying to wake up. I had to say I felt better.

Next was Math class once again with Mr. Ohm. I normally enjoy Math. It can be tricky but it always makes sense. It follows a pattern. Patterns are comforting. That day though, in fact, all week we were studying units of measure. Practicing converting metric to non-metric and Celsius to Fahrenheit.

I mumbled under my breath, "Why can't the whole world just use the same systems! After all, it's just different ways of labeling the same stuff!"

Apparently, I said it louder than I had intended because several kids stared in my direction. Mr. Ohm looked at me and nodded. "Good point, Lia. Maybe when you're older you can work on uniting the world."

I heard somebody laugh. I knew it was Wendi.

"Maybe I will," I said. "Maybe I will!"

My final morning class was English with Ms. Bliss. The name really doesn't describe her well at all. Ms. Bliss is OLD. I mean she taught my mom English. She always wears her white glowing hair up in a bun. I also believe she thinks of her English class as the most important class in the school, if not the country, if not the world, if not the Universe. She gives so much homework, it's unbelievable. She likes to say, "Kids today have it too easy. It's my job to toughen them up for the real world…."

For homework, yesterday, she told us to read the first three chapters of The Lion, the Witch, and the Wardrobe. Fair enough. I guess she is the teacher. But she gave us a pop quiz on it this morning. The quiz covered the first four chapters and it was going to be added to our final grade!! Ms. Bliss said she did it because "A good student will do more than what they are told!"

I didn't know how I went. I just knew I only read the first three chapters. And of course, it was an essay test. I couldn't have been happier when the bell rang for lunch so I could get out of there.

Lunch Break...

Lunch time was my favorite part of the day, the part where I could hang out with my friends. Plus, while the cafeteria was painted the most disgusting shade of green, the food was surprisingly tasty. Jason, Tim, Krista and I were sitting at a table together, talking about nothing and everything all at once.

"Emily looks so pretty with her hair like that," Krista commented.

I chewed on my mouthful of pasta. It wasn't quite as good as my mom's but it came close. I nodded to Krista. "Yeah, I love it short on her as well. It suits her so much!"

Jason and Tim talked about action movies. Funny to see Jason get so excited as they disagreed over the greatest movie ever.

"Diehard, man," Tim said.

"Nope, Princess Bride!" Jason insisted.

Lunch wouldn't be complete without Wendi strolling by our table; Brandon on one side and her best friend, Lori on the other. Lori plays defense on our team and she may be the toughest girl in the world.

Wendi looked down at my plate. "Good to see you chose the veggie salad with your pasta. You'll need the energy for our game this afternoon."

"Right!" Lori grunted.

"Nice to see you guys again," Brandon said with his usual perfect smile.

Wendi pulled him along to their cool kids' table.

Now Tony was challenging kids to arm wrestling for a dollar. After dominating one table he set his sights on us.

"Hey, either of you loser dudes feeling strong and

lucky today?" he smirked.

Tim took a deep breath, I knew he was getting ready to stand, but I spoke up, "Tony, Jason will take you on."

"He will?"

"I will?" Jason replied.

I nodded to Jason. "You can do this, you've been studying judo under Sensei Joe."

"Yes, but Judo isn't arm wrestling," Jason argued.

"Plus, you play lacrosse every day!" I added.

"Yeah, but it's not arm wrestling!"

I shrugged. "It's all about leverage."

I stood up and gave Tony my seat across from Jason. Tony plopped into my seat, put down his elbow and opened up a meaty hand.

Jason shot me a look that said, *are you crazy?*

I gave him my look that said, *you can do this!*

He reluctantly put his elbow on the table and locked hands with Tony. Tony's hand engulfed Jason's.

I bent over. "I'll start you guys on three.... One,

Two…" I reached down and gently pushed on Tony's arm right behind his bicep, between the elbow and shoulder. I'd taken enough martial arts in my day to know there was a pressure point there. If I gave that spot the right amount of super pressure it should totally weaken Tony's arm. "Three!" I said quickly.

Tony gritted his teeth and tried pushing Jason's arm down. To pretty much everybody's surprise (most of all Jason's), Jason's arm didn't move back at all. Instead, his arm pushed forward, driving the arm of a very shocked Tony to the table.

"I win!" Jason shouted tossing his arms up in the air.

Tony sat there, mouth wide open.

"Careful Tony, you don't want to swallow a fly," Tim joked.

We'd caught the attention of almost the entire café and just about everyone laughed.

Tony got up, an irritated smirk on his face. "Oh, whatever!" He ducked his head and hurriedly scurried away.

I almost felt sorry for Tony. Almost. But I felt so good about myself that I chomped hungrily on my veggie salad. "Man this salad is great!" I beamed.

"Yeah, it really is good," Krista said. "Only I have to avoid it because the raw cabbage and broccoli can give me gas," she whispered in my ear.

Oh, I had forgotten about that. Still, maybe raw cabbage and broccoli wouldn't affect me. We talked for a few more minutes. And then suddenly I felt an all too familiar urge in my stomach. Uh oh, I knew I needed to get out of that room, and outside. Fast.

The Fart...

I rushed up to the supervising teacher, Mr. Khrone, who sat at a table next to the double doors leading in and out of the cafeteria. Mr. K was a big bald man with a softly spoken voice.

"Mr. K I have to get to the bathroom fast!" I said in a rush. "Personal lady problems," I added blushing.

Mr. K turned redder than my face felt. He handed me the hall slip. "That's okay, take your time," he replied.

I knew if I went directly outside that would cause suspicion. I took the slip and headed towards the girl's bathroom. There were two things that I'd always noticed when I went to that bathroom. It was painted a pretty shade of light blue, which was so much better than the ugly green that the rest of the school was coated with. Also, and more importantly, each of the stalls had a little window cut into the wall. I assume it was for ventilation but today, those windows would most likely save the school.

I raced inside, my heart pumping furiously in my chest. Breathing a quick sigh of relief, I realized I was lucky (for once) as the place was empty. I decided on the middle stall and locked the door behind me. Turning towards the wall, I looked at the window just above the toilet. It wasn't a big window but it would work. I leaped up onto the toilet and reached for the handle. It happened to be one of those windows that pulls open just to let some air in or out. I pulled the window and it dropped open about a quarter of the way. But I was definitely not going to fit through that space. The window may have been built to only open part way but it wasn't built to stand up to super strength. I grabbed the handle and yanked down. The window's metal framework fought me for a second and then gave in. I pulled the window completely out of the frame and fell to the floor, the window in my hand. It could have been worse, I could have fallen into the toilet. Or I could have let my gas out right then and there and somehow, I didn't think that would be a good idea at all. It was just lucky that so far I'd managed to hold it in.

I jumped back up on the toilet, held my breath, and my stomach, and slid out the window; once again being careful to hold back my gas. Being outside was good but I knew I needed to get as far away from the school as possible. Glancing urgently around the school's backyard, I noticed the lacrosse practice field was empty. That would have to do. I jumped up in the air and leaped a good hundred feet with that jump. "Wow!" I exclaimed loudly to myself. "That was pretty cool!"

A couple more super jumps and I found myself in the middle of the empty field. Time for my release. I turned away from the school just to be safe. That was when I noticed a herd of cows maybe 100 yards away. They looked at me and began to moo. "Sorry cows!" I said. "I have no choice."

Then I let out my fart. It felt good. The fart made just a little PUT sound. If I'd stayed in the cafeteria, most people probably wouldn't have even noticed. Sniffing the air, I noticed it didn't seem that bad at all. Maybe Mom was exaggerating. Then I realized I could no longer hear the cows behind me. When I turned around, I saw the entire herd laying on the ground, legs up in the air. Using my super vision (which I just found out I had), I saw they were still breathing. But man, I had clobbered them, "Oops!" I said. "Yeah, people would definitely have noticed that!"

I leaped back to the school and climbed through the space where the bathroom window had been. I returned the window back into the frame. Next would come the hard part, going back out and interacting with my classmates knowing one fart and I could drop them all. It was a kind of weird feeling of power tinged with total embarrassment.

Just as I left the bathroom I ran into Krista.

"Phew, you're okay!" Krista said. "We were starting to worry. Usually, you don't take that long!"

"Oh, I'm fine!" I assured her. "That broccoli and cabbage just got to me…"

She put her arm around me and we headed back to the cafeteria.

"See Lia, I told you, that's a dangerous combination!"

"You have no idea!" I replied.

The second half of school day...

After the craziest lunch period in the history of lunch periods, I had history class with Mr. Paradise. Mr. Paradise was one of those teachers who loved to talk and talk and talk.

He would practically glow when lecturing about history, always telling us, "You need to know history so history doesn't repeat itself."

He went on and on about the people in history who abuse power. He told us how "power can corrupt...." It was the kind of a talk that hit home, especially now that I knew I could fart and be the only one left standing in the classroom. Mr. Paradise must have seen me staring off into space, thinking about how I can't let this power get to me.

"Lia, you look like you're giving this a lot of thought," Mr. Paradise commented.

I snapped back to the moment. "Ah, yes, actually I am."

Mr. Paradise smiled. "Good, you should. You all should. You all have your own power and skills. At this age, you are just coming to learn what your powers and gifts are.

After all, you need to understand your own unique powers before you can use them wisely in the world!" Mr. Paradise tended to get a bit poetic. A lot of kids thought it was weird to talk that way. Usually, I did too, but today his words hit home.

Art with Mrs. Brown went smoothly. It was a day for oil paintings on canvas. Mrs. Brown put an apple and an orange on a table in front of the class.

Our assignment was to simply draw those and have fun. Mine looked like a red blob alongside an orange blob. The two kind of smudged together to a reddish orange blob.

There are some things that super powers just don't help with. When I looked over at Jason's, I saw that his painting looked like a real-life apple and a real-life orange.

"You have incredible talent," I told him.

"Thanks," he smiled.

Mrs. Brown appeared and looked over our shoulders. She took in Jason's near masterpiece and said, "Miss Strong is correct, you do have talent!"

Jason beamed.

Mrs. Brown turned her attention to my painting. "Art is about enjoyment," she said. "Did you enjoy this?"

I nodded. "Yeah, I kind of did."

Mrs. Brown grinned. "Then good job."

Computer class with Mr. Swimmer happened to be another class that Jason really stood out in. I swear he could make a computer sing – literally! He wrote a program where you could type in a phrase and the computer would sing it.

Mr. Swimmer was amazed. In fact, even Tony Wall walked over, put his hand on Jason's shoulder and said, "Good job dude!" I smiled at that. Apparently, Tony, like most bullies, would respect strength. I felt a little better about using Jason to humiliate him during lunch. As Mr. Paradise would say in history, "Throughout history people have believed the end justifies the means." In this case, it might have.

My school day ended with yet another humbling experience, French class with Madame Broch. I have no idea why, but whenever I attempt to speak French my tongue seems to get tied up in knots. I thought maybe having a super tongue and super coordination would help. But no such luck!

"Bonjour, comment allez-vous?" Madame Broch asked me as I entered the room.

"Be end Mercy," I answered, my tongue twisting over the easiest words.

Madame Broch rolled her eyes just a bit. "Nice try, dear," she sighed in English.

Yep, it was now official. I may have super powers, but I was still just an average kid who happened to be really strong.

At the end of the school day, Jason and I met at our lockers to collect our gear for practice. Jason played on the boy's lacrosse team. It certainly wasn't a love for him but like he would say, "the running is good."

Plus, it gave us a chance to hang out and walk home together after school.

As we were collecting our sticks and pads, Ms. Janet, the janitor, walked by sweeping the floor. I like Ms. Janet a lot. She's a retired army sergeant who now cleans the school in the afternoons.

"Hope you kids have a good afternoon!" Ms. Janet smiled.

"You too!" Jason and I both replied together.

"After I leave here I get to go clean a few more houses," she added with another smile.

"Ms. Janet, why don't you enjoy your retirement more?" Jason asked.

She grinned. "I enjoy working. It makes me feel useful. Besides, these days any extra cash I get goes to help my grandkids in college." She shrugged. "Well, nice talking to you kids. Have a good practice. These floors won't sweep themselves, so I'd better get to it."

I thought for a second about using super breath to blow all the dust out of the school, but I didn't. I wasn't sure I could control my power enough to do that. Besides, Ms. Janet seemed to really enjoy her work. So, I guessed I should leave her to it.

Boy, I was tempted though!

Practice Makes Perfect...

After school, I met Krista on the lacrosse field for practice. I actually enjoy our practice sessions. I liked working out with the team and also the way we learned to cooperate and work as one. I even love doing drills. Wendi, being the star of the team, hated drills, she just loved to scrimmage. So of course, she managed to talk Coach Blue into an all practice scrimmage session.

And of course, before we started, I got a text from Mom.

MOM> Remember to be careful at practice!

I knew this would be a test of both my abilities and my patience.

Coach Blue broke us up into two squads. The first was basically Wendi and Lori, and all the biggest girls against Me, Krista, Marie and all the smaller, quicker girls.

"They definitely have a size advantage on us!" Krista whispered to me as we lined up to start.

"Don't worry, we have speed and brains on our side!"
I told her.

"Okay, ladies, I want this to be minimum contact!"
Coach Blue warned. "After all, you are all on the same team
so we don't need you beating each other up."

Lori snickered.

"So, what we're going to do is…each team will take a
turn with the ball. If they score or miss, the other team
brings the ball up the field." Coach pointed to Wendi.
"Wendi's team will get the ball first!"

Coach Blue blew her whistle with all her might. I
swear she loved the harsh sound it made. Wendi grabbed
the ball, ran down the field, dodged a couple of our
defenders then quickly shot the ball into the back of the net.
She raised her arms in victory! Lori came over and gave her
a high five and a chest bump.

Shannon, our goalie, tossed the ball to me. I started
running up the field. A couple of Wendi's teammates lunged
at me. I dodged them easily, as they seemed to move in slow
motion. I darted up the field. I'd never felt so sure and
confident. I just knew I was going to score. I ran past two
more defenders as Wendi shouted. "Somebody stop her!"

Too late, I had already closed in on the goal. I flicked
my wrist and rocketed a shot over the goalie's, right
shoulder. I smiled. I shot that just hard enough to get past
her without it being so hard, it was dangerous. I felt I was
really catching on to my powers.

"Wow, I barely saw that!" Michelle gasped. "Nice
shot, Lia!"

Wendi picked up the ball and grumbled something
about luck, and even how a blind squirrel finds a nut now
and then. Wendi passed the ball to Lori. Lori passed back to
Wendi. The next thing we knew they had scored again.

Shannon tossed the ball to Krista. Krista threw a long
pass to Marie. Marie noticed I was open and hit me with a
perfect pass. I caught the ball and tossed it in the goal in one

fluid motion.

Krista and Marie ran up and patted me on the back.

"Wow, you're playing so amazing today!" Marie grinned.

"You are on FIRE!" Krista shouted.

"It's just the great teamwork," I insisted. Deep down, I had to say I felt amazing, like nothing in this world could stop me.

Wendi walked by, intentionally hitting me in the shoulder. I barely felt it but I still moved my shoulder like she had affected me. Wendi hit the ball out of the goal and glared at Michelle.

"Can't you stop anything, girl?"

Michelle shrugged. "Hey, I'm a good goalie but that was just a better shot."

Wendi looked at Lori. Lori nodded. I didn't like the look or the nod.

Wendi took the ball and headed back up the field. She flicked the ball into the net but this time she didn't celebrate. She reached into the goal, grabbed the ball with her stick and tossed it to me.

"Okay, Strong, let's see how strong you really are!" she said.

"I like a challenge," I replied.

I made my move up the field. Wendi ran behind me. I wasn't running full speed but neither was she. I didn't know what she had planned. Still, I kept my eye focused on the goal. I also knew I didn't want to score this goal. Okay, I did want to score this goal. I wanted to score so bad. Then I could taunt Wendi. But I knew I needed to pass the ball around. Not only was that being a good teammate but it also didn't make me look too suspicious.

I snapped a quick pass to Krista. Hearing footsteps coming at me from the side, I turned to see Lori closing in on me full speed, stick up. I lowered my shoulder just as Lori rammed into me. Lori went flying over me and then crashed to the ground out cold. I fell to the ground too, even though I barely felt the hit.

Coach Blue blew her whistle. "Time out! Time out!" She ran out onto the field. "You girls alright?"

I sat up. "I'm fine coach…"

Lori laid there on the ground. Marie tapped her gently on the arm. "Lori, Lori…"

Lori lifted her head up. "Anybody get the number of that truck that hit me?"

"That was a dirty hit by Lia!" Wendi insisted, jumping up and down.

"Looked clean to me," Coach Blue said. "One of the rare times she didn't agree with her star."

Lori sat up. "Coach is right. It was a clean hit." Lori gave me a thumbs up.

I walked over and helped her to her feet.

For the rest of the practice, we ran drills. I learned that my power is certainly fun to use, but I had to be on my guard always!

That was something I definitely had to watch out for!

Snack Break...

After practice, Jason, Krista, Tim and I headed to Mr. T's Donuts & More. Mr. T's was the big hang out for middle school kids. The place had everything we needed, comfy couches, free Wi-Fi, yummy snacks, and the best milkshakes in the world. It even had an old school retro type pinball machine. Everyone loved the place!

The four of us sat on a couch munching on our food. I had a strawberry donut that I was washing down with chocolate milk. The smooth taste of the milk made me so glad that I wasn't lactose intolerant. I knew some people who were, and they couldn't have any dairy products whatsoever. I would have hated not being able to enjoy milk without releasing a fart that would drop the entire room.

"Man, it looked like you were having a great practice," Tim said.

Jason chimed in. "I would have loved to see the look on Wendi's face when you tossed in all those goals."

"Oh, she was so not happy!" Krista added.

"I just got lucky guys," I said with a smile.

No sooner did we mention her name then Wendi appeared at the door with Brandon and Lori in tow.

They walked by our couch. Wendi stuck her nose in the air like she hadn't noticed us. But Lori looked at me and at least gave me a nod. I took it as a gesture of respect. Brandon actually smiled and stopped to talk. My heart skipped a beat when he said, "Lia I saw you from our practice field, you were playing so well. Keep it up!"

Wendi stopped and acknowledged we existed with a, "Oh hi..." She pulled Brandon along, "Come on, Brandon lets go to our couch."

Before I had time to think about what just happened,

something weird hit me. I got a funny feeling in my stomach. No this wasn't going to be another super fart (thank the stars) this was something else. Like I just knew something bad was going to happen. Looking out the big windows that lined the wall at the front of Mr. T's, I scanned downtown Starlight City. We were right across from the SLC Bank. Sure enough, I saw two men in hoodies getting out of a big black car parked right in front of the bank. A third man, also in a hoodie, sat in the driver's seat with the car running. They were going to rob the bank! Nope, that was not happening, not on my watch.

I got up and grabbed my book bag. "Sorry guys, I need to go to the bathroom."

"Want me to come?" Krista asked starting to rise.

I smiled and shook my head. "Nah, it might be safer if you don't."

"Got it," Krista said dropping back to her seat.

I moved to the bathroom as quickly as I could without moving at super speed. My heart pounded away in my chest like a beating bass drum. I couldn't tell if it was because I was nervous or excited. Probably a little of both.

I went into the middle stall and closed the door. Somehow, I had the feeling there were going to be a lot of bathroom visits in my life from now on. I looked up to see a window at the back of the stall. Not a huge window but one I could fit through. Now I needed a disguise.

Rummaging through my book bag I found an old black tutu from a dance recital I did at the start of the year. I also pulled out a white ski mask. For once, the fact that I never cleaned out my book bag was a good thing. I quickly changed into my new outfit. Sure, I didn't look stylish but nobody would be able to identify me. Or at least, I hoped not. Because that was the important thing right then.

I jumped up on the toilet (after making sure it was closed) and popped open the window. I slipped out the window and promptly fell into a big garbage can in a side alley. Yep, I really should have looked before I leaped or dropped in this case. Feeling the squishy goo under my feet, I decided I didn't want to know whatever the heck I was on top of. I pulled myself out of the trash bin and spun around as fast as I could, causing most of the slime and trash to spin off me. I took a deep breath. It was Go time! I only hoped I could handle it. For a brief moment, I considered texting my mom. But no, there was no point in worrying her. I knew I could handle this. I was a Strong woman – literally and figuratively. I had taken enough karate lessons that I knew how to fight. I just needed a plan. Not to leap in feet first this time because that's how people get hurt.

I surveyed the scene. The driver was tilting backward and forwards nervously in his seat. I noticed smoke billowing out of the tail pipe. I smiled. I had my plan.

Not on my watch!

I leaped across the street landing right behind the old black smoking sedan. I bent down not only to hide but to cripple the car. I grabbed the exhaust pipe in my hand. I couldn't tell if it was hot. If it was, the heat didn't bother me. I pinched the pipe closed like it was made of putty. No way would this car go far at all.

I leaned back and ducked behind the car. Now I just had to wait for the other two guys to come out. From the chaos I could hear inside the bank, it wouldn't be long.

Seconds later, the two masked men burst outside the front doors of the bank. One of them, a bigger man, turned back into the bank and shouted, "If nobody follows us, nobody gets hurt."

He leaped into the front seat of the car. The other man jumped into the back seat.

"Drive, drive!" The bigger man ordered, waving his gun around like it was a conductor wand.

From the spot where I'd been hiding, I had a clear view as the car pulled away from the curb. It sputtered and jerked forward. Then it coughed a stream of black soot out the back.

"Drive faster!" the big man ordered the driver.

With my super hearing, I could hear every word that the men said. Their voices were a mixture of frustration, anger, and fear.

"I'm hitting the gas as hard as I can!" the driver said, shaking and panicked, "I've got no idea why this car is moving so slow…"

The car stammered and sputtered to a stop.

"What the?" the big man said.

"Maybe we don't have gas?" the man in the back

offered helplessly.

"I put ten bucks worth of fuel in before we came here!" the driver said.

I reacted fast. Jumping forward, I grabbed the front and back passenger doors. I pulled them off the car like they were made of plywood.

"What the?" the big guy repeated once more.

I leaned into the car and grabbed him, then rammed his head up into the roof of the car. He went limp. I pulled him out of the car and dropped him to the curb. The guy in the back seat aimed his gun at me. I shot forward and grabbed the gun's nozzle. Pulling the gun out of his hand, I crushed it into a ball of metal. The man lunged forward in desperation and punched me in the nose.

He pulled his hand back wincing in pain.

"Now that was rude!" I said, changing my voice to sound very official. "Plus, kind of stupid since I bent your gun like nothing." I leaned over the back seat and pinched him on the shoulder. He crumbled over.

Turning my attention to the driver, I stared at him as he stood there with his arms up in the air, shaking. He handed me his gun. "I give up!" he gulped.

I took the gun and squished it. "Smart man!" I told him. "Still, I need to make sure you don't run away!"

"I won't! I promise!" he said, crossing his heart with his fingers.

As if I could believe a guy who just seconds ago, was perfectly willing to rob a bank. I reached forward and tapped him on the forehead. His head rocked back, his eyes rolled to the back of his head then dropped shut. He plopped back in his seat, out cold.

Reaching for the ignition, I turned off the car. I then backed out of the car and leaped up into the air towards the alley.

The New Normal...

When I returned to the dining area of the restaurant, everybody was still gathered around the front window. By then, the police had come and were taking away the battered bad guys. Jason's dad, who was chief of police, talked to the local press.

Jason was bursting at the seams when he saw me. "OMG! You missed it! You missed the most awesome thing!"

"It wasn't that awesome!" Wendi insisted.

"What did I miss?" I asked, pretending to be completely ignorant of what had just gone on.

"Some super girl stopped the robbery!" Brandon gushed. "She totally clobbered those three bad dudes. I wonder if she's good looking…"

"If she was pretty, why would she wear a mask?" Wendi asked.

"Probably to hide her identity," I answered, far more defensively than I would have liked.

"Could you please turn on the TV, Mr. T?" Jason called out. "My dad is speaking now."

The TV in the corner of the room popped on. Mr. T flicked a switch to the local station and there stood Jason's dad, looking all tough and official in his best and bluest uniform. "These men are three of the five Hanson brothers," Jason's dad said. "The other two are still at large but we will get them."

"What about the news that some sort of super girl overpowered these three and saved the day?" the reporter asked.

The chief hesitated for a second. He drew a deep breath. "Well, while we do appreciate the help of ANY citizen to make our town a better, safer place…. I can't condone the actions of a vigilante."

"But she did save the day!" the reporter insisted.

I fought back the urge to say, you go girl.

The chief nodded again. "Yes, she did, and we appreciate it. But one of the Hanson's, the oldest named Bart, is threatening to sue the city. He says she used excessive force plus he is demanding to be reimbursed for the price of the guns she destroyed."

"That's ridiculous!" I said under my breath.

Jason heard me and agreed.

Krista, Tim, and a few others also nodded in agreement.

"That is a good point," Wendi admitted. "The girl might be strong…but she certainly isn't that smart, and definitely, has no sense of style!"

Brandon shook his head. "I still gotta wonder if she's cute…"

Wendi elbowed him in the stomach, an annoyed expression on her face.

Brandon bent over then straighten himself up. "I'm sure she's not as cute as you."

I considered saying, I bet she's way cuter. But then decided I had enough going on right now. No need to start upsetting Wendi. Besides, she was my teammate and captain, we needed to work together. Not only would that be better for the team but it would make my life easier. Having super strength didn't protect me from the mean comments of other girls. My skin might have been tough as steel but I still had emotions, normal kid emotions. I needed all the friends I could get. And while Wendi might not ever be a friend, I certainly didn't need her as an enemy.

Suddenly my train of thought was broken by my stomach rumbling. And by rumbling, I mean really rumbling. It sounded so loud it actually shook the couch we were sitting on. I threw my hand over my stomach and felt my face turn bright red. "Oops, sorry!" I apologized, slinking down a bit. "I'm just so hungry."

"You had a long hard practice," Jason told me. "Let's get you some food." Jason signaled for Mr. T to come over. Mr. T, a small bald man, was not only the owner but also the waiter and chef at the restaurant. He and Mrs. T, his tall, redheaded wife, pretty much ran the entire place themselves.

"What can I get for you kids, now?" Mr. T asked.

"I'll have another shake, a triple burger and a mega order of fries," I grinned.

Mr. T smiled. "Long practice or are you excited about seeing that Starlight City now has a super hero?"

"A little of both," I replied.

"I'll just have fries and onion rings," Jason said. "Don't want to ruin my dinner."

"Chilly dog for me with extra onions!" Tim beamed. "I'm starving as well."

57

Mr. T. smiled. "I guess you don't have a date tonight."

"If he keeps eating like that he's never going to have a date!" Jason chuckled.

Mr. T. turned to Krista. "And for you?"

"Just a salad and a glass of water," Krista said. "I need to watch the calories."

Mr. T. took our order and walked off.

I turned to Krista. "Krista, your weight is fine. You look great!"

Krista looked away from me. "Yeah well, I felt a little slow on the field today. Watching you, I was in awe. You moved so fast like you were a totally different speed to me." She sighed. "Maybe Wendi's right? Maybe I do need to shed a few pounds."

Now, this was a side-effect of being super that I hadn't thought about. I hadn't considered that my performance might make my friends feel bad. Wow, this super stuff could be super complicated. I put my hand on Krista's shoulder and looked her in the eyes. "Krista, you're perfect just how you are!"

"Do you two need to get a room?" Tim kidded.

I shot Tim a look. He dropped back in his seat. "Sorry, bad time to make a joke." He gulped. He looked at Krista. "But she's right, you know. You look good."

Jason nodded in agreement. "Yeah, Krista, Wendi is just jealous of you, cause you're so naturally pretty."

Krista smiled, her face blushed a deep shade of pink. "Thanks, guys... you guys are the best friends a girl could have."

"Want to share my fries?" I asked.

"Deal!" she replied, the wide smile returning to her face.

A few minutes later the food arrived at our table. Never had food smelled or looked so good. I guessed it was due to my new super senses. Plus, my stomach hadn't stopped quietly rumbling. I could see that using my super strength was demanding. I dove into the food, eating as fast as I could, while still trying to have some manners.

"I'm impressed," Tim said, watching me eat a triple decker hamburger in a few bites.

"I've never seen you eat like this," Jason frowned, a curious expression on his face. "And I've known you forever."

"Must be low blood sugar from practice!" I told him. I picked up the shake. My instinct was to guzzle it down in one gulp. But I had to fight that instinct back. Instead, I took a small sip. My taste buds jumped for joy and it took all my willpower to put the shake back down on the table. *Breathe in between bites and gulps*, I reminded myself. Being super doesn't mean being a super hog. My stomach still craved more food. I had an urge to open my mouth and eat all the fries with one gulp. But no, I could control this. I had to control this.

Reaching over, I grabbed one fry only and popped it into my mouth. I savored the flavor and the texture. Sure, I was hungry but no need to rush into quenching this hunger. I was a Strong woman mentally and physically. I finished my snack at a leisurely pace, enjoying both my friends and my food.

Yes, I could do this super thing! At least I was pretty sure I could do this super thing. I just needed to be careful. I could be careful. All I had to remember was to breathe, and think before I leaped.

Cat in tree...

After our rest stop at Mr. T.'s, Jason and I walked home. By then, Jason was practically bursting at the seams.

"Too bad you missed that super girl! She was awesome!" he was shaking his head in amazement.

I nodded. "I'm sure she was....but why are you so happy about it?"

Jason stopped walking and looked at me. "I thought you knew me better than anybody."

"I thought so too," I said. I stopped to think for a moment. My eyes popped. "Oh, you're happy that Starlight City has a super hero just like in the comics!" I replied quickly.

Jason grinned. "Yep! It's so good! The way she took care of those three Hanson Brothers like that. Wow! My dad tells me those Hansons are really bad dudes."

"Can't imagine your dad saying, *dudes*," I said in return.

Jason shook his head. "Well no, not in those exact words. But they are bad guys! Bad to the bone, he says. He also says they're not to be messed with. According to him, they aren't very bright but that makes them even more dangerous."

"Yeah, I can see that," I nodded in agreement. That was something that had stood out clearly.

"But here's the amazing thing. This girl, this super strong girl, took them out like they were nothing. And she ripped the doors off the car like they were toy doors."

"Well remember, Wendi thinks this is all some sort of reality show trick or a commercial," I looked at him, trying to be convincing.

Jason shook his head again. "Nope. No way would

my dad be involved in anything like that. This girl is legit!" He looked up into space. "I wonder if she has a boyfriend."

I nudged him (extra gently) to move forward. "Come on, let's get home."

"Yeah okay," he said, moving again. "Why would a girl like that ever be interested in me anyhow?"

"Because you're smart and caring!" I answered sincerely.

He smiled at me. "Thanks. But smart and caring isn't cool. How about way, way handsome?"

I shrugged. "You're okay. Though you may want to work on your modesty some," I teased.

Before Jason could say another word, I heard a muffled sobbing from across the street. Turning towards the sound, I saw our little neighbor, a cute seven-year-old, named Felipe, sitting on his porch steps crying.

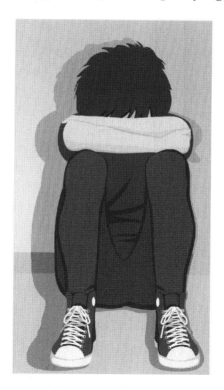

"Now that's not normal. Felipe's the happiest kid I've ever seen!" Jason said, a look of concern crossing his face.

I started across the street. "Come on, let's go see what's wrong." Hearing Felipe sobbing like that broke my heart. I had to fight back the urge to move at super speed to see what was bothering him so much.

Felipe saw us coming and wiped his tears. He didn't want us to know that he'd been crying. I guess boys are macho from a really early age.

"What's going on Felipe?" I asked, bending down to him.

He glanced at me and shook his head, but I gave him an encouraging smile and he spoke. "I'm worried." His sad face was streaked with tears.

"About what?" Jason asked.

Without taking his tear soaked eyes off us, he pointed to a big oak tree in the yard. "My cat, Bella is stuck up in the tree. Way up in the tree. And she's too scared to come down. My mom called the fire department but they can't come yet. I'm so scared she'll fall before they get here."

Jason smiled and tried to comfort him. "Don't worry, Felipe. Cats hardly ever fall and even if they do they land on their feet."

"Yeah but hardly ever isn't never," Felipe said. "Plus, landing on their feet doesn't mean it wouldn't really hurt!" he added. Felipe was a sharp kid. I had to admit that he had a point.

Looking over to the tree, I noticed it was big and thick and covered with leaves. The tree had to be over a hundred years old. Using my super vision to zero in, I saw Bella the cat, sitting on one of the upper outer branches. How had she managed to get herself way up there? I probably could have leaped up to grab her but no way I could do that without giving myself away.

Part of me wanted to wait and let the fire department

handle it. But a bigger part of me said that helping a crying seven-year-old was just as important as stopping a gang of crazy robbers. This might have even been more important. I mean, come on, what's better than making a little kid happy?

I started walking towards the tree. "Don't worry, Mr. Felipe I will get the cat down for you!" I said confidently.

"You will?" Felipe and Jason both said at once. I'm not sure which one of them sounded more amazed.

Felipe stood up to follow me. Jason followed Felipe. "How?" Felipe asked.

"Yeah, how?" Jason asked.

I reached the base of the tree and looked up. "I've been studying trees...." I said.

"You have?" Felipe asked.

"When?" Jason added.

I looked at both boys. "I like to read about different things on the internet sometimes. Usually on my phone," I replied vaguely.

"Oh, she means when she's in the bathroom, trying to get out of class!" Felipe concluded.

Yep, like I said, Felipe was a sharp kid.

Jason looked up, shading his eyes from the sun. "That cat has to be at least twenty feet up. How are you going to get him down?"

Putting my hand on the tree I told them both. "It's a little-known fact that if you hit a tree in the right spot, the tree will vibrate just enough to shake its branches. I can make the branches shake so Bella drops from the tree."

Felipe gulped.

I touched Felipe gently on the shoulder. "Don't worry, when she drops I'll catch her before she hits the ground. She'll be fine, I promise!"

Jason stood there, arms crossed, eyes squinting. "So you're going to make a giant tree shake and then catch a falling cat?" his eyebrows were raised in disbelief.

"Yep," I answered.

He leaned in and whispered to me. "You know, even if you somehow manage to shake a big, thick, sturdy tree like this, it would still be really hard to catch a falling cat from that height."

I nodded. "Don't worry I can do this," I assured him.

"You do realize that even if you manage to catch this cat, this cat is going to be very scared and lash out with its sharp claws!"

I nodded again. "I'm aware of that." I looked at Felipe's hopeful face. "But it's a risk I am willing to take."

Jason stared at me for a moment or two. He sighed. "If you actually think you can do this then I believe you. What can I do to help?"

"Just you and Felipe stand back by the house so I have room to move," I replied.

"Okay," Jason agreed. He hesitated for a moment before ushering Felipe back to the porch.

I looked at the tree. I looked up at Bella. I knew shaking the tree wouldn't be the problem. The trick would be shaking the tree just enough so I didn't knock the tree out of its roots. Plus, I wanted Bella to drop but not go flying. This would take some knowledge of physics and a lot of luck.

I slowly approached the tree. I looked up at Bella. Yes, she was still way up there. I peeked back over my shoulder at Felipe and Jason. Felipe was biting his nails and Jason had his arm around him. That was sweet. I told myself to concentrate. I could do this. I just worried that hitting the tree would cause a lot of damage. Then, like a lightning bolt, the answer flashed into my head. I didn't need to hit this tree. I just needed to puff a bit of super breath upwards, into the tree. I could direct that force much more easily.

First, I puffed a breath into my hand, just to make sure I didn't have super bad breath. After all, I wanted to knock Bella from the tree, not knock her dead. My breath smelled of salt and French fries. I smirked. No way that would be dangerous.

Next, I put on the show for Jason and Felipe. I very, very gently tapped the tree while looking upwards. But then I inhaled and then exhaled up towards Bella. The force of my breath knocked some leaves flying and jarred a surprised Bella up and over the tree. She went flying towards the house, paws clawing away in fear and shock.

I shot past the tree hoping Felipe and Jason were paying more attention to the now flying cat, rather than me. Positioning myself between the tree and the house, I stood right beneath the falling Bella. Reaching up, I caught Bella with two hands. I breathed in, making sure I closed my hands softly. Bella scratched and clawed through my school uniform. I couldn't blame her, she was scared and in shock. I cradled her into my body.

"Calm down, Bella," I whispered. "You're fine now."

Bella suddenly stopped struggling. She started to purr. Nestling her head under my arm, she fell asleep with what appeared to be a contented smile on her face. She then began to snore.

Jason and Felipe rushed over to me.

"Thank you! Thank you!" Felipe said hugging me.

"It was nothing, I told him." I handed him his sleeping cat. "I guess the experience tired her out. She'll be fine in a couple hours!"

"Thank you! Thank you so much!" Felipe repeated. "I'd better get Bella back into her bed so she's nice and safe." He turned and headed into his house, humming happily all the way.

"That was amazing!" Jason said with an astonished look on his face.

"Ah, it was nothing," I insisted.

The Big Reveal...

Jason looked at me, his face flushed with color. I could hear his heart racing. "Seriously! That was incredible!"

I shrugged. "Ah, just luck..."

Jason shook his head in denial. "No way! Those were some crazy skills. How the heck did you know that about trees? And how in the multiverse did you catch a falling cat?" Jason noticed my sleeves had rips in them from Bella's claws. "Oh, that had to really hurt."

He reached for my arm. Without thinking, I let him check it. He rolled back my ragged sleeve. It felt so nice to have Jason care about me like this. "Your sleeves are ripped to shreds..."

"Yep, cat claws will do that," I said proudly, still not getting it.

"But...but...your arms... they're perfectly smooth. Not a cut or scratch on them!"

That's when I got it. I pulled my arm quickly away. "Just lucky again, I guess." My heart was hammering. Did he suspect something?

Jason's mouth dropped open. "OMG!"

"OMG, what?" I coaxed, my stomach churning anxiously.

"You are her!" Jason said, his face a mask of shock.

"Her who?"

Jason pointed at me and started walking slowly backward. Not out of fear, but out of amazement. "You're the super strong girl!"

I laughed. "Don't be so silly!"

Jason kept walking backward and going over the events in his mind. "It all makes sense...first, you have the amazing practice, Lori plows into you and gets annihilated, then you disappear when Super Girl comes out... you come back when she disappears...then you eat a super amount of food." He was piecing it all together, one event at a time. This was not supposed to happen!

"Jason you're being ridiculous," I giggled nervously. "You've been reading too many comics!"

He stopped walking and stood stock still in the middle of the road, locked in thought. "My best friend is super!" he exclaimed loudly. "This is soo cool."

I shook my head. "Jason, I wish I was super but I'm not..." Before I could complete the sentence, I spotted a car speeding down the road directly in Jason's path.

The driver, a kid not much older than Jason and I, had his eyes downcast, probably looking at his phone rather than the road. No way could I let Jason pay for the driver's mistake.

Suddenly Jason heard the car rushing towards him. He turned to the car and froze in his tracks. I leaped through the air and landed between Jason and the oncoming car. I held Jason back with my left arm and extended my right towards the speeding vehicle. By then the driver had seen us and jammed on the brakes. The car started skidding to a stop but it was still going way too fast. I leaned forward with my right arm and jammed it into the hood of the car, forcing the car to a dead stop. The air bag popped out. My hand left an impression in the hood of the car. The car attempted to push forwards but I didn't allow it to budge.

"Put the car in park!" I ordered the driver, who stared at me, his mouth open wide in terror.

I felt the car stop trying to resist me.

I then reached over and pulled the hand print impression out of the metal of the car. All the while Jason stood there, stunned with disbelief. "Jason get across the street!" I told him, my voice full of authority.

"Right!" he said, and without hesitating, did as he was told.

I walked up to the driver. He sat there rigid and speechless. The air bag had deflated but he didn't move an inch. He looked up at me. "I…I don't know what happened…. I just looked away for a second…"

"Yeah, that was way dangerous!" I told him.

He lowered his head. "I know. I'll never look at my phone while I'm driving again." He shivered with fear. His face was ghostly white. "Are you two alright?"

I nodded. "Yeah, we got lucky!"

The kid shook his head. "I have no idea how I ever stopped the car in time. You sure you guys are okay?"

"Yes, we're fine," I nodded.

"Wonder why the airbag went off?" he asked.

I shrugged. "Probably just some sort of safety precaution."

He frowned with confusion and then agreed, "Yes, probably a safety precaution!"

"We won't tell anybody this happened, if you don't tell anybody this happened," I stared directly at him.

He looked up at me, his face filling with relief. "Believe me I don't want anybody to know I screwed up like this. My parents would have a massive fit!"

"You promise you'll keep your eyes on the road from

now on?" I asked. I made it sound like a question but it was more of an order.

He nodded. "Oh, I so promise! I never ever want to be scared like that again."

I trusted him. I had certainly made an impression. "Okay just be careful. There are a lot of small kids in this neighborhood!"

"Right, got it!" he agreed, nodding his head, his face still a pasty white.

He waited for me to join Jason on the other side of the street. Then he started up the car and drove off, giving us both a small wave.

I looked at Jason and saw that his expression was full of pride. It was not the face of a guy who had almost been hit by a car.

"Why are you smiling like that?" I asked. "Weren't you scared?"

"No of course not, you're my best friend and I know you've got my back!" he answered confidently.

I shook my head. "Jason, you almost got run over by a car. You have to be more careful. Only dumb luck kept you from getting killed."

"It's not luck," Jason insisted. "It's amazing! My best friend is super! This is the coolest thing ever!"

Between friends...

"Holy cow!" Jason continued on, "I can't believe you're the girl who stopped the bank robbers. And then you just saved my life!"

I lifted a finger. "One, I can't believe you just said, *holy cow*." I put up another finger. "And two, you can't really believe that I'm super..."

Jason looked me in the eyes. "Lia, you just stopped a speeding car with one arm! And you put a dent in the car. A big dent! You can't deny being super. Cause seriously, that ain't normal!"

"Don't say ain't!" I told him.

"Just making a point," he grinned.

I sighed. My sigh knocked him backward.

I lunged forward, holding him up, "Oh Jason, I'm so sorry."

He laughed as I steadied him. "Look! You just breathed on me and I went flying!"

"Well not FLYING," I insisted. I couldn't stop a smile from appearing on my face.

"Girl, you are super!!" he began jumping up and down.

I rolled my eyes. "Don't call me girl!" I insisted.

He steadied himself. "Okay, okay. I got a bit carried away. After years of comic reading, I am actually best friends with a super being. This has got to be the best day of my life!"

In a way, I couldn't help but feel relieved that Jason had figured it out. Not only was he my best friend in the world, but he was also a comic and super hero expert. He could help me understand all of this better. He could help me find my new place in this world. Plus, maybe he could help cover for me if I needed an excuse. After all, in the movies all superheroes had confidants; people they could rely on, to help them. Jason had always been mine. So, it was perfect that he could be a part of this.

I nodded, finally admitting the truth. "Yes, I am super..."

He leaped into the air. "I knew it! I knew it!!"

I gently put a hand on his shoulder to calm him. "Remember it's a secret. Right? I don't want anybody else to know. Mom says if I tell people they would want me to do things for them."

"That makes sense," Jason agreed. "So your mom is super too?"

I nodded. "Yep, afraid so!"

He beamed. "Well, that explains why your grandma and great grandma are so fit. They must be super as well?"

I nodded again. "That's what mom tells me. I guess all the Strong women are well, way strong."

"Why didn't you tell me this sooner?" Jason asked, eager as could be.

I lifted my hands up. "I didn't know until yesterday."

He looked at me. "You kept this from me for an entire day!" He turned away, a hurt expression on his face. "I thought we were friends!"

My heart started to race. I couldn't bear the thought of losing Jason over this. Touching him gently on the shoulder I said, "Jason....I...."

He turned to me, grinning widely and waved me off. "Just teasing you, Lia! I totally get the idea of keeping a secret identity."

I breathed a sigh of relief. Once again, sending Jason staggering back a little.

"Oops, still don't know my own strength."

"That will take some getting used to," Jason realized the obvious.

"Just be glad I didn't have onions or garlic for lunch,"

I told him.

He laughed. "So, exactly how strong and tough are you?"

I shrugged my shoulders. "No idea," I paused. "Mom seems to want me to learn by doing. I know I could squish a gun like it was nothing. It felt like putty in my hands. And I knocked out those Hansons with a tap."

"Plus, you have really powerful breath," Jason added. Then a sly smirk passed over his face. He pointed to his garage. "Let's say we give you a test or two."

"Sounds like fun!" I told him. I was so glad that he'd found out. I knew my mom wouldn't be thrilled, but I also knew she would understand and trust Jason, just like I did.

Testing...

Jason's garage was filled with weights, exercise machines, punching bags, and dummies. His dad, the chief, happened to be very big on staying in tip top shape. He always told Jason and me that a good cop's best weapons were his mind and his body, in that order. Guns were messy and a good cop never had to use one.

First Jason set up a weight bar for me. "How strong do you think you are?" he asked.

"No idea," I replied honestly. "Strong enough to stop a car and pull doors off a car. I also pulled one of the Hanson guys out of his car like he was nothing."

Jason grabbed a couple of big weight plates and put them on the bar. "My dad only has 500 pounds of weight. We'll start with that," he grinned. "If it turns out to be too heavy, which I am guessing it won't be, then I'll remove a few plates."

"Plates? They look like weights, not something you eat off." I said, kind of joking.

"We're going to have to work on your witty comments. They're not that funny!" He chuckled anyway.

Standing up on a concrete platform, Jason made sure the weights were steady. After locking in the right and left sides, he walked to the middle of the weight bar and tried to lift it. It didn't budge. "I can't even begin to lift this weight. So I can't help you."

I hopped up on the platform. Something inside of me, I don't know what, told me I wouldn't need Jason's help. "That's okay," I assured him. "Just to be on the safe side though, you'd better stand back, in case I lose control."

I knew I was being extra cautious because once again I could tell this was going to be very easy. I also somehow knew it would be safer for Jason to stand back.

He reluctantly moved back to the other side of the garage.

When I figured he was safe, I reached over and grabbed the bar with my left hand, then hoisted it over my head like it weighed nothing. I smiled proudly. I also smelled something, something like two-day old cheese mixed with a skunk. That odor emanated from my left arm pit. It definitely had a kick to it, but surely it wasn't that bad? I looked over at Jason. His eyes rolled to the back of his head and he dropped down as stiff as a board. I lowered my arm down and locked my arms to my sides. I guessed that the thought of Jason getting hit by the car had caused me to burn through my deodorant.

"OMG! I just killed my best friend with super B.O!" I thought. Now that was a phrase I'd never expected to be saying to myself!

I stared at Jason and saw his left foot begin to twitch. His chest began to rise up and down. I hadn't killed him after all. He was probably lucky I'd only lifted up one arm. My first thought was to run right to him. But then I figured if I did that, a whiff of me from up close might REALLY kill him. I jumped off the platform and grabbed my bag. Ripping open the bag, I pulled out my special deodorant. Before applying it though, I blew on each of my underarms hoping to force the sweat and stink off. I coated my skin with deodorant.

Then I raced to Jason's side. Kneeling down beside him, I gently shook his arm. "Jason, Jason!" I coaxed.

His eyes slowly opened. "Wow, did you get the number of that train that clobbered me?"

I shook my head in dismay.

He sat up. "That was crazy! I've never been hit that hard in judo or lacrosse. My head is still spinning." He hesitated for a moment and then smiled with realization. "So, that's what they mean by seeing stars."

"See! This power of mine is too dangerous!! You got knocked silly by one whiff of my armpit from across the room! If I lifted both arms you might have died. Nope, no more power for me!"

Jason laughed. "You're so funny when you panic." He grinned at me encouragingly. "Look, Lia, you have this power for a reason. Sure, you're going to have to learn to control it. But I know you can do it."

"What makes you so sure?" I asked.

"Because I know you, you can do whatever you put your mind to!" He patted me on the shoulder. "It's obvious you're way super strong. And I don't have nearly enough weights to test you. So, let's try the treadmill and punching bags instead."

"You sure you want to keep doing this?" I asked, frowning.

He stood up with my help and winked at me encouragingly. "Of course I do! I was born to do this kind of thing. I've been waiting my whole life!"

I reluctantly agreed but made sure to take care this time, and continued training under Jason's watchful eyes. First, he asked me to run on the treadmill. After hooking me up to the heart monitor, he set the tread to move at the highest speed and resistance. I started moving my legs in rhythm. In less than a minute, I had the treadmill churning faster than the speedometer could measure. The bottom of the treadmill began to ooze smoke.

"Stop! Stop!" Jason shouted, waving his hands in front of me.

I slammed my legs down through the pad of the treadmill and the tread stopped moving. But the machine kept smoking. "Oops!" I said, hopping off the machine.

Jason grabbed a fire extinguisher and sprayed it down. "I think I can fix this. Luckily my dad never uses this machine, so it should be okay. Meanwhile, I think we can determine that you are way fast."

I nodded. "Yeah, I guess that's a safe bet."

Next, we moved to a big heavy punching bag dangling from the ceiling. Jason pointed to the bag. "This is the heavy bag, take it easy with it."

I curled my hand into a fist and gave the bag a light tap. It went flying off the hinges and crashed into the far wall.

"Oops!" I said for the second time.

"OMG!" Jason's face was a mixture of surprise and shock.

Looking over my shoulder I explained to him. "Yeah, that's why I only tap people to knock them out."

He shook his head adamantly up and down. "Yep, that's smart."

I walked across the room and picked up the punching bag. Hoisting it up on the hinge, I patted it down, smoothing it out. It didn't seem that beat up and looked like it had barely been used.

Jason gave me a solid metal bar which he actually had

trouble lifting.

"So, what do you want me to do with this?" I asked. "It's not heavy at all."

"Twist it!" Jason ordered.

I promptly went and tied the bar into a knot and then another knot. I displayed it for Jason by balancing it on one finger and popping it up and down.

"Okay, stop showing off!" he laughed. "Now please put it back to how it was."

I untangled the bar and put it back on the floor. Then I looked at my phone. "This has been fun, Jason, but it's getting a bit late and I have homework to do. I'd also like to clean up a bit before Mom gets home. She's going to want to talk about my day. I'm sure she won't be thrilled to hear you know about my powers."

"But I'm cool!" Jason said.

"Yeah, let's hope my mom agrees!" I answered with a smile, but a worried feeling was creeping into the pit of my stomach.

"Oh, BTW, you better start thinking of a name for your alter-ego. Super Girl is what everyone is familiar with in the DC comics. Is that what you want to be called?"

"Okay," I replied with a nod. I hadn't even thought of that. But I figured sooner rather than later, the media would name me.

Heading home...

On my way home, I noticed a heap of birds on the ground, in the area around Jason's garage. They appeared to be shaking. After a closer look, I quickly figured that they must have been blasted when I blew the smell off my underarms. I really did have to be careful with my powers and just hoped that the birds would survive!

I heard a familiar voice shouting, "Hold the bus. Hold the bus!!"

Looking down the street with super vision, I saw Jan, the janitor running towards a city bus. The bus had started its engines and was getting ready to take off.

I couldn't let that happen. I knew Jan had not only served our country in the past but she had worked way hard today. I needed to hold that bus. I just had to do it carefully, without being super if I could. I was quite certain I could hold the bus in place, but I had to be more subtle-like. I needed to use my head here.

I leaped forward to the bus, but instead of grabbing it, I walked up the stairs towards the driver, a short skinny woman.

"Swipe your bus pass please," she said, pointing to a scanner next to her.

"Okay," I replied reaching into my book bag. "I'm sure it's here somewhere!" Looking over my shoulder, I saw Jan closing in on the bus but I still needed more time. I dropped my bag on the floor. The bus driver rolled her eyes as I began to search through my pockets. First, I pulled out my side pockets. Then I pulled my wallet out of my back pocket. I slowly started going through each item. "Will my school ID help?" I queried slowly.

The bus driver shook her head impatiently.

For a second, I thought about searching in my shoes, but then I got worried I might I have super stinky feet that would knock out the entire bus. While it would keep the bus in place, it would also defeat (or defeet) the purpose of holding it for Janitor Jan.

"Girl, do you have a bus pass or not?" the driver demanded.

"Must have left it at home," I apologized. "Can you wait?"

"No!" the driver said firmly.

I heard Janitor Jan's footsteps on the road nearby. I nodded to the driver and hopped off the bus. Just to be safe, I put my hand up on the door so the driver couldn't close it.

Janitor Jan reached the bus door. "Lia, what are you doing here?" she asked me, panting.

"Just holding the bus," I explained.

"Thanks, Lia!" I could hear the gratitude in her voice. "It's been such a crazy long day, I'm so glad I didn't have to walk home."

I smiled as I watched Janitor Jan get on the bus. The door closed and the bus drove away. I felt good about myself. I had solved a problem without using super powers. Well, without really relying on them.

Feeling more pleased than ever, I headed for my house.

Home Sweet Home...

I got home and dropped my book bag on the floor. Plopping down on the couch, I pulled out my phone. Shep came over and licked me, tail wagging. He could sense I'd had a long day.

"Thanks, Shep, nice to know I can always count on you!"

I had to admit I was dying to see what my social media feed had to say about the super girl or whatever they were going to call me. Turned out most people were calling me Super Teen. Not sure how they could tell I was a teen, but I kind of liked the name.

As for the comments, they were mostly positive.

Super Teen is way cool.

She took out those bad Hanson Brothers like they were nothing.

Man, I wish I could rip doors off cars.

If I was her I'd use my powers to rob the bank. Well, okay I'd be tempted.

There was already a hashtag #SuperTeenRocks

I had to admit that made me feel awfully good. I was becoming famous. Sure, I was becoming famous in disguise but that was okay. I knew they were talking about me. Plus, I was doing my thing to help make the world better. As well, I could still live a normal life. Well, at least as normal as I could, being super.

Then there were the questions asking who the girl was, and of course negative stuff that mostly came from Wendi. In the previous hour, Wendi had tweeted or posted:

I think she's fake.

She must be ugly because she doesn't show her face.

It's easy doing good when you have super powers.

Let's talk about something real. How about our practice? That cheap hit Lia put on poor Lori!

That last comment got to me a bit. Wendi just couldn't admit that somebody else was good at something. But I felt my anger drop when I saw Lori's comment.

Wendi, cut it out! That was a clean hit by Lia. Stop talking bad about one of our teammates!!!

Then there was another comment…

Seriously, it's great that both you and Lia played so well. Your team is going to dominate!

I beamed as I read that one, as it was from Brandon. It was so cool that Brandon not only noticed me but also thought I'd played well. Brandon, the best-looking boy in school, if not the world, had defended me. I felt so good, I could have floated off the couch. But then a couple of city warnings popped into my news feed bringing me back down to earth.

"Two Hanson Brothers remain at large!"

"Citizens who spot either of the two should IMMEDIATELY contact the police. Captain Michaels."

"These men should be considered armed and dangerous. Their capture should be left to the professionals."

I knew that last comment was aimed at me. Speaking of comments aimed at me, a text popped in from my mom.

MOM> Just got out of surgery. I saw what you did. Part of me, the Strong part is proud. The Mom part in me says, Be careful! Love Mom.

I texted her back.

LIA> Don't worry, I'm always careful!

A fly started buzzing around my face. The fly darted back and forth, first to my face then around my feet. It seemed to be circling me, kind of taunting me. Even its buzz, buzz appeared to be a challenge.

When it hovered around my feet, I kicked my shoes off. They had been on all day and I was dying to get them off. I just didn't dare do it when there were any other humans around.

The fly instantly stopped buzzing, it nosedived to the floor.

"That's what you get for messing with me!" I told the fly. Looking down at Shep who was now sleeping, I thought, *Oops! Lucky he didn't get a direct hit!*

I stood up, picked up the fly off the floor and headed to a window. Mom's plants in the window sill had wilted. One of them was a cactus. *Oh my gosh,* I thought as I opened the window and tossed the fly out. *My smelly feet can wilt a cactus.* I knew three things: this was going to get me a speech from Mom about using my power wisely. I needed a shower badly. And lastly, it was definitely a good thing I hadn't taken my shoes off in public.

Heading up the stairs, I decided I should take a very long shower.

Shower interrupted...

When the water from the shower hit me, somehow it felt better than any shower I had ever taken. I finally understood what Mom meant when she talked about water washing away any tension. I made a concerted effort to make sure I really scrubbed my underarms, feet, and toes and between each toe. If it could smell, I washed it well. From now on that would be my motto:

If it can smell, wash it well....

Okay, it wasn't exactly "Up up and away!" or "To infinity and beyond!" This would be more of a private motto. I'd work on the more flashing one later.

I heard a weird ringing sound coming from the sink outside the shower. I kind of recognized that ring. Moving the shower curtain aside, I glanced across the steaming room to see my phone flashing. Somebody was actually calling me! Not texting, not snap chatting, not tweeting me. Somebody wanted to talk to me the old-fashioned way. This had to be important.

I jumped out of the shower, wrapped a towel around myself and grabbed the phone. When I saw Jason's name and image with the wording, incoming call, I hit the speaker button.

"Jason, what's up?" I asked.

"Turn on your TV, put it on channel 13 news," Jason had a sense of urgency in his voice. He was normally calm and cool. (Except of course when talking about comics.) So this had to be important.

Walking into my room I grabbed the remote and flipped my TV on. I punched in channel 13. A local reporter appeared on the screen. She was at the Starlight City city zoo. Yeah, the name was a bit silly but that wasn't what mattered right then.

"Breaking news from Starlight City city zoo! There is a seven-year-old boy who has somehow fallen into the gorilla pit. The boy has been approached by the zoo's pride and joy, a 20-year-old male gorilla name Henry. Zoo officials and police are trying to determine the best way to handle the situation. They can't tranquilize the gorilla because the sedative will anger him before it relaxes him. They are afraid to shoot Henry because he has the young boy in his arms."

The camera zoomed in. There was my neighbor, sweet little Felipe in the arms of a massive gorilla.

"Oh, this is so bad!" I said to Jason over the phone.

"You gotta get him out of there!" Jason pleaded. "My dad and his men are there but I'm afraid they could do more harm than good. I'm betting you could free Felipe from Henry without Henry *or* Felipe getting hurt."

I thought for a split second while looking at the screen. Felipe was staying surprisingly calm. It looked like he was talking to Henry. Henry, for his part, seemed fascinated by Felipe. I knew though, Henry could crush Felipe by accident. Gorillas had to be extra careful around humans. I could relate, but I was pretty certain Henry didn't quite grasp that concept.

"Okay, I'll put on a disguise and get there asap!" I told Jason.

"Thanks, Lia!" Jason said, sounding relieved. "I'll bike there."

"Jason..."

"Don't worry, Lia I'm not going to try to be a super hero, I'll be there so I can run interference for you if you need it!"

"Thank you, Jason!" he truly was a sweet great friend.

I spun around really fast to spin dry myself. It worked so well. But I needed some sort of costume. I went into my closet and pulled out a red pair of tights that I'd worn to a dance recital the previous year. When I tried them on, I found that they still fitted. Ripping through my drawers I found an old pink mask that I'd used when trick or treating as a kid. I popped it on. It also still fitted. I then tossed on an oversized white t-shirt that came almost to my knees, and a pair of white canvas sneakers. Costume complete. It wasn't fancy, but it worked.

I needed a way to get to the zoo without anybody seeing me. The good news was, our house was centrally located so nothing in this city was far away. The tricky news was, I couldn't just walk or run or jump there without attracting attention. I went to my window and looked out at the neat houses lining our street. I had it!

I pried open my window and jumped from the window to our neighbor's roof. From there on, I jumped onto the next roof and then the next and the next, until I came to the end of the street. Luckily, I had a good sense of direction. Even from the rooftops, I knew where the zoo was and what my next jump should be. On the roof of the house at the end of the block, I needed to leap across the street so I could head off in the other direction. This would be a tricky leap. I needed to leap far, and land without doing damage to the house.

Bending my knees, I pushed forward and leaped up in the air higher than I thought I ever could. I flapped my arms a bit, not really sure why I did that. In mid flap, I figured I had a better chance to glide than to fly. Duh. I held my arms out straight. I over shot one house but landed face first on the house after my target. The distance was impressive even if the landing wasn't. I stood and leaped again and again from roof to roof.

The zoo soon came into sight. I had to say that was quite the amazing way to travel. Of course, now came the tricky part, getting into the gorilla pit unnoticed and without scaring Henry. I may not have been an expert on gorillas. In fact, all I knew was from a TV show I'd watched while back. But I did know that scaring a big 400-pound gorilla wouldn't be a good thing at all.

I jumped into the zoo's parking lot. From there I could hear all the commotion coming from the pit. I coiled and jumped, over the zoo's fence. I then landed on the ground right near the gorilla pit and leaped again. This time, I landed in the back end of the pit and had a clear view of Henry. He had put Felipe down but still had one giant hairy hand wrapped around Felipe's arm.

Felipe remained quite calm as he spoke to the ape. "Ah, Mr. Henry the ape, I didn't mean to come down here. Sorry. Some big ugly guy pushed me. Now if you let me go, I'll leave..." I could sense Felipe fighting back the tears.

Slowly, I made my way towards Henry and Felipe. I had hoped Henry would be able to sense my power like other animals.

Felipe noticed me before Henry did.

"Are you here to help me?" he asked.

I nodded.

He smiled happily. "Wow, Super Teen is here to save me!"

Okay, news of my name sure traveled fast.

"How did you know that?" I asked Felipe. "This is my new outfit, so you couldn't have recognized me."

He smiled. "Who else would come down into a gorilla house to save me?"

"Great point," I replied, slowly walking towards Henry.

Henry had his massive hairy head tilted. He, liked most of the human onlookers above us, really had no idea what to make of me. I showed Henry my open hands.

"Henry, I am here to help," I said slowly and surely. "I know you only want to take care of Felipe since he fell into your home. That's very nice of you. But I am here to take Felipe back to his mother and father so they can take care of him." I used my most calming soothing voice.

"I don't think he speaks English," Felipe told me.

"Yep, I know that, but I'm hoping he can feel my emotions and feelings," I told Felipe.

"You big kids can be weird sometimes," Felipe said with a shrug.

I drew to within an arm's reach of Henry. Henry pulled back and put both arms around Felipe possessively. The crowd above gasped.

My super hearing picked up Chief Michaels' voice. "Great! We finally had a shot but now we've lost it. This is what happens when amateurs take matters into their own hands."

I also heard Jason defend me by saying, "Give her a chance Dad, I know she can save Felipe without hurting the gorilla."

"Come on Henry," I said slowly. "Let the boy go. His Mom and Dad need him." I held open my arms. "You can take me, instead. I could use a big gorilla hug."

Henry looked over his shoulder at me, thick bushy eyebrows raised. He seemed to be taking in my words. Well if not my words, then my sentiments.

"Let the little boy go, Henry." I coaxed with my words and my eyes.

Henry released Felipe from his grip.

88

I jumped forward and hugged Henry tightly. I needed to make sure he didn't grab Felipe again so I tightened the bear hug I had locked on him.

"You okay?" I asked Felipe, turning towards him.

He nodded. "Yes. Thank you, Super Teen!" He gave me a huge grateful grin. Now that was sweet.

I lifted Henry off the ground. "I'll take him back to his home area now. You wait here for the people to come and get you."

"Okay!" Felipe agreed, the smile on his face faltering as he watched me begin to move away.

Then something Felipe had said to Henry jumped into my mind. "You said you were pushed in here?" I asked.

Felipe nodded. "Yeah, by a couple of really big men. One was talking to my mom and the other pushed me in. I heard them say they needed a distraction."

OMG! It had to be the Hansons. They were going to rob the zoo. Listening with my super hearing, I somehow managed to pick two far off voices out of the crowd. They were talking about getting to their car and making a smooth getaway.

First things first though. I needed to get Henry nice and safe into his cage. I patted him on the back and started carrying him slowly to the end of the pit area. There were a couple of handlers in the enclosure who had been unsuccessfully trying to coax Henry back.

Henry started to fight me but I tightened my grip. "Just relax Henry!" I ordered. "You may be strong but you're going to lose this if you fight me."

Henry instinctively became calm. I guess he finally felt my power. I carried him over to his handler and put him down gently in the cage. The people above clapped.

Through the noise, I heard Jason say, "See Dad, I told you she could do it!"

"You were right, son!" he replied.

It made me so happy to hear their words. Still, there was no time to bask in the glory. I had two Hansons to catch. And I was angry. How dare they risk a young boy's life so they could rob a zoo!

I leaped out of the pit over the crowd. I realized that this was just like the dream I'd had. One super leap and I was in the parking lot. I saw a black van starting to speed away. Nope, not going to happen. Those nasty Hansons had gone way too far. Time for me to put a stop to them once and for all!

The Bad Guys...

Using my super vision, I spotted two men in the front seat of the black van racing out of the parking lot. They were laughing and seemed quite proud of themselves. Only total jerks would be pleased about putting a young boy in an enclosure with a real-life gorilla, just so they could make a few bucks.

I leaped across the parking lot. I dropped in front of the speeding van and held out both arms. "You bad boys better stop if you know what's good for you!"

"Hit her!" the Hanson in the passenger's seat ordered.

The driver slammed the brakes. "No! We're thieves, not killers!"

Hitting the brake had slowed the car down some but not much. It still slammed into my outstretched arms. The car crashed to a stop, the hood crinkled up like tin foil.

The two brothers popped open their doors and headed off in different directions. I sighed and pushed the broken car away from my body. It went tumbling across the parking lot towards a bunch of parked cars. Oh, rats! I didn't take into account how strong I really was, especially when angry. Not wanting to let the flying escape car damage innocent peoples' cars, I jumped back into the air and over the ruined van. Landing just beside it, I caught the van a mere few inches before it hit the row of parked cars.

Just then, I heard something behind me. I turned to see one of the Hansons charging at me with a big lead pipe. I shook my head as he rushed at me screaming, "ARRRG!" at the top of his lungs.

He smashed the pipe over my head. When he pulled it back, it had a head shaped dent in it. He looked at the pipe then he looked back at me. Tossing the pipe over his shoulder, he took a boxing position.

"You really aren't smart at all. Are you?" I said to him.

I held out my jaw and as I expected, he foolishly punched me in the chin with an upper cut. When he pulled back his hand, it was throbbing red. "You broke my freaking hand!" he shouted at me.

Shaking my head I told him. "No, YOU broke your hand, you idiot!"

He pointed at me with his good hand. "I'm going sue!"

I shook my head. "No, you're not! First of all, you're a mean, nasty crook. Second, I hate to break this to you but you have no idea who I am."   I tapped him on the head with my pinky and he crumbled to the ground. Looking down at him I added. "Third, when you're conscious again, you might not even remember what hit you!"

I turned my attention towards the last Hanson brother as he ran out of the zoo. Pulling off my left shoe, I tossed it across the parking lot. It flew through the zoo entranceway and hit the fleeing Hanson in the back of the neck. He fell to the ground face first. I couldn't help but smile as I leaped across the parking lot towards him. It was important to make sure he'd stay down and I also needed to get my shoe back. That shoe could be a public hazard. Even before I was super those shoes could stink up a room.

In a couple of bounds, I was behind the last of the Hansons. My shoe hitting him in the back of his head had stunned him but it hadn't knocked him out. I bent down and picked it up. He was a big burly bear of a man. He was unshaven and had to weigh over 300 pounds. I walked up to him. "Stay down and be nice and quiet for the police."

He started to push himself up off the ground.

"I figured you wouldn't be smart enough to do as you were told!" I shook my head at him.

"The police aren't taking me!" he bellowed. "No…"

I held my foot under his nose and he instantly stopped talking. Wriggling my toes, I gave him a nice whiff of my foot. After a mere half hour in my canvas shoes, it was enough to make his eyes roll to the back of his head. He then turned blue, and I heard him mutter the words, "Wow, what power...."

His head plopped straight down in the dirt. He'd be no problem for the police. It looked like he'd be out cold for days.

I popped my shoe back onto my foot and leaped up into the air to bounce back home.

A long day done...

Climbing through my bedroom window, I found my mom sitting on my bed watching TV. It was still tuned in to channel 13 news.

"And there you have it, folks! Super Teen not only saved seven-year old Felipe Moore from the zoo's star attraction, Henry the Ape, she also carried Henry into his cage unharmed. Then the super teen somehow figured out the last of the Hanson brothers had robbed the zoo. This powerful teen easily overpowered two dangerous thugs. One of them is still unconscious, and as one of the medics put it, 'he's in dream land.' I for one, am happy we have this super team looking out for our interests in Starlight City."

Mom flicked off the TV. "Busy first day, I see?" She patted the bed.

I sat down next to her. "You mad?" I asked her.

Mom smiled and put her hand on my shoulder. "How could I be mad about you helping people and an ape?" She took a deep breath. "I'm proud and worried... mostly proud. It does seem like you're doing a good job with your powers. I know it can be tricky!"

I shook my head. "Tell me about it. I had some nervous sweat when Jason almost got run over by a car. It burnt through my deodorant like nothing. Then I thought I'd killed him when I lifted my arms while he was testing me on his dad's sports equipment."

"Wait, Jason knows you're super?"

I nodded, anxiously, not sure how she was going to take that news. "Yeah, he figured it out, Mom. He's so smart." I tried to gauge her reaction before trying to explain further. "But I'm glad he knows! It gives me somebody to talk to that's my age. Plus, I hate keeping things from him.

Plus, he's the one who told me Felipe needed my help. Plus, he stood up for me when his dad was complaining about me. Plus, he knows a ton about comics and super heroes so he's a great resource."

Mom smiled weakly. "That's a lot of pluses, Lia. It sounds like your powers are developing really quickly. But then I guess you are the 20th Strong woman to be born. Legend has it you could grow to be the strongest of us all."

"Wow!!" I exclaimed. "Really?"

She nodded. "Not sure how reliable the legend is, but you are certainly off to a great start. We all get super strength and durability but some of us develop other powers. Like my mom has heat vision, especially when she's angry. I have x-ray vision that comes in really handy as a doctor."

"Okay, x-ray sounds weird but creepy," I told her.

She laughed, "It's handy once you get used to it." She paused for a moment before continuing. "How about super pheromones? Have those popped up yet?"

"Not entirely sure what those are?"

"Your scent has a way of making people like you a lot. It makes them more willing to do what you say. I don't have that power, but your great grandma does."

"Ah, that's why all the men are always giving her their jello."

Mom laughed. "Yes, she does love her jello."

I thought for a moment. "Jason did act weird after I accidentally knocked him out with underarm odor. Plus the last Hanson mumbled some freaky stuff after I waved my stinky toes under his nose. So maybe…"

"Well that's another tricky power, but one I'm sure you can handle."

I smiled at the idea of being able to make people do my bidding. Now that could come in all sorts of handy.

Mom put one hand on my shoulder and looked me in the eyes. "I recognize that look. Your great grandma looks like that before making people cluck like chickens."

My smile grew. "Yeah, now I understand how she does that cool trick. It's like hypnosis."

"No, it's way more powerful than hypnosis. A hypnotized person won't do anything against their will. A person under pheromones' influence will do pretty much anything to please. You have to promise to be careful IF that develops more."

I nodded. "Check! Got it, mom! You can count on me. What other powers can I get?"

She looked at me. "The list is pretty long and extensive. There's the basic freeze breath. Some of our great grandmothers could move things with their minds and even make themselves fly. One could scream and shatter rock. One even had acid burps."

"Gross," I said. "I wish there was a manual."

Mom stood up. "Actually, I have something better." She darted away at super speed. Less than a second later, she sat by my side holding a book. "It's nice to finally be able to show you my true self," Mom said. She handed me an old leather bound book. I opened it up. The title page said: A History of the Strong Women.

"Each of the last 19 Strong women has left notes in this book. It's a history of us…"

I started flipping through the pages. The first ones were dated 1650. I knew from doing a genealogy paper at school that's when our first ancestors arrived here. Not only in this country but in Starlight City. My great, great, great, great, great, great, great, great, great, great, great, great, great, great, great, great, great, great, great great grandma was one of the original founders of this city. Even though I'd hardly ever bragged about it, I still felt proud of it. Wendi told everyone how her family had been here for 300 years. I knew she'd have a fit if she learned mine had been here longer. Either that or she'd call us all losers for not being able to get out of this city. With Wendi, you can never win. That's why I never brought it up. I was just happy to know we'd been a part of this city from the start. Now holding this book in my hand, I felt closer to my ancestors and prouder than ever.

Mom stood up, a beaming smile on her face. "Okay, today is a very special occasion, so I'm cooking your favorite meal tonight!"

I sniffed myself. I did have a bit of nervous odor about me. "Should I take another shower?"

She shook her head. "Nah, it's just us Super Strongs tonight. Right? Much rather have you spend the time hitting the books, or maybe even have a night off!"

"That sounds good!" I grinned.

Just as she left my room, my phone vibrated. It was a text from Jason.

JASON> Man you were AWESOME!

LIA> Thanks, Jason.

JASON> I knew you could do it! I knew you could!

LIA> I'm glad one of us did :-)

JASON> Lia! U were super b4 U were super!

LIA> UR dad doesn't seem to think so....

JASON> He thinks Lia is great. It's just he's not used to the other part of you. Don't worry he'll come around.

LIA> I hope so!

JASON> Trust me. C U tomorrow for our walk to school. ☺

LIA> Wouldn't miss it for anything! If you need any help with your French homework let me know :-)

JASON> Oui Oui (that means yes yes...)

LIA> Ha! Ha!

A wonderful day...

Mom cooked my favorite chicken casserole with broccoli on the side. Some kids found it weird but I actually loved broccoli, especially smothered with my mom's cheese sauce. Mom assured me that when cooked, broccoli wouldn't make either of us lethal. I told her about my fart and how I clobbered a herd of cattle. "You should have seen them, Mom. They dropped like they were fleas. And then I had to double check they were still breathing. Thank goodness they were okay. I'd hate to be responsible for harming a herd of cattle!"

She laughed and told me, all in all, I had handled everything well. She also said that as I matured I would learn more control. Mom explained that she could hold her gas in now and only risked letting it escape when she was in a safe zone on her own somewhere. She said she'd also used it once at the cinema. A bunch of people in the theater wouldn't stop talking so she released a silent fart. She put the entire place to sleep for the duration of the movie.

I laughed so hard at that story. It was the funniest one she'd told me so far! After that though, we talked about normal things: school, work, friends, boys. Although, I changed the subject back to school when she asked if I had any crushes. That was just too embarrassing. But like mom said, we may be superhuman but we're human first.

Because it was a special day, Mom let me off having to clean up the dishes. So, I went to my bedroom to check my Facebook news feed. There was a heap of comments about Super Teen from kids at school as well as lots of people I didn't know. Most of them were really positive...

Wow, she's amazing.

To think we have a superhero here in our town!

Nice to see her saving the day.
I wish I had her powers.
Glad she saved Henry and the boy!
Man, she is fast.
Did you see how high she can jump?
Her disguises are cool!

I especially liked that one. Of course, there were some negative comments as well and Wendi's name was attached to a couple of those.

That girl is so over-rated! And besides, she seems dangerous!

A couple of other people were also unimpressed...

Kids these days shouldn't take the law into their own hands.

One of the Hansons claims she beat him with super foot odor – gross.

But that was what some people thought was the best superpower of all. A few even wished they had super foot odor themselves because they could have so much fun with it. Krista commented that she'd love to have the shoe store all to herself! Hmm, that was a good idea.

I went to bed fairly pleased with myself. It had been a crazy day. It may very well have been the best day of my life. I learned I could make a difference in the world. A big difference. Sure, it might be tempting some time to knock out the mall and go on a wonderful shopping spree. But I knew I could fight back those temptations and do the right thing. Well at least do the right thing more often than not.

I drifted off to sleep. I dreamed of leaping up into space and looking down on Earth. I noticed a big green asteroid heading towards our planet. I flew to it and caught it, stopping it in its path. Then I pushed the giant green rock back out into space. I flew back down to Earth to be greeted by a huge parade. Everybody loved me.

Suddenly I woke up and smiled. Now that was a cool dream. I wondered if I could ever get that powerful, able to fly in space and stop asteroids. Wow! Before I could ponder the question for too long I heard a noise coming from down stairs. Looking over at my phone the time was 2:22 am. I sat up and listened.

Pat, pat, pat…it was the sound of footsteps, downstairs. They weren't mom's footsteps. Too heavy. Not Shep, because he was asleep on the floor by my bed. The person was trying to be quiet but they couldn't muffle their steps from my super hearing. I stood up, tossed on a robe and headed down the stairs.

There in the living room stood a man holding a flashlight.

"Dude, you picked the wrong house to break into!" I said.

The man turned his flashlight on me. "No, wait!" he said. "This isn't what it seems…I'm a friend!"

The man did look sort of familiar. I leaped towards him. I landed right in front of him. "Sorry, friends don't break into their friend's houses."

The man smiled. "My, you truly are amazing!"

I grabbed his big flashlight and squished it in my hands. "Talk or you're next!" I growled.

The man's smile grew. The smile somehow made me feel at ease like I had seen it before.

"Look buddy. I don't know what games you're playing but you're not going to get me to like you!"

"But…" he said holding up a hand. "You're needed…"

I tapped him on the forehead and he crumbled to the ground. "Sure I am, buddy!"

The lights in the living room popped on. I turned, ready for anything. I saw Mom coming down the stairs. "What's going on here?"

I lifted up the man's unconscious body. I showed him to mom. "I caught this jerk breaking into our house!"

Mom walked slowly towards me. Her eyes popped

open. She knew this man. She smiled at me. "I can't believe it…" she said.

"What?" I asked, shaking him like a rag doll. "You know this creep? I can tell you know him!"

Mom nodded. "I do know him. I used to know him quite well. You do too, in fact."

She bent down and gently touched him on the forehead. "He has aged, but that's to be expected."

"Is he a bad guy?" I asked, even though Mom didn't seem to be treating him like one. "He made me feel some emotions. It was weird."

"No, he's not a bad guy. In fact, I believe these days he works for the government," she explained.

"Mom, who is this guy?" I asked.

She looked at me and spoke. But never in a million years did I expect the words that came from her mouth.

"Lia, this is your father…."

***

Find out what happens next in…

Diary of a Super Girl – Book 2
THE NEW NORMAL

Available NOW!

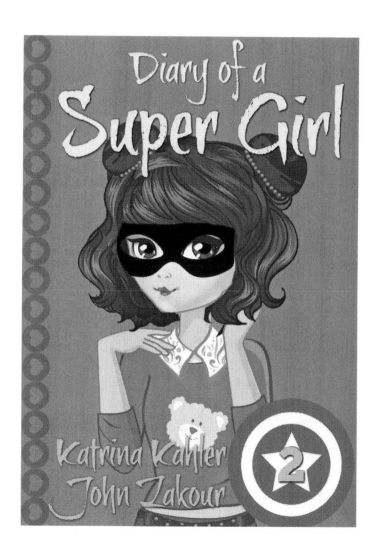

Want to read about some strong women in history?

The history of and words from the Strong women (Lia's ancestors) ...

Born in 1650: Alice

Talents: **super strength**

Accomplishments: The first

Words to Those Who Follow: **Be true...**

Thoughts: My parents wanted a boy, what they got was a girl stronger than any five boys. I had to keep my strength secret so people would not think of me as a witch. Perhaps I am a witch of sorts. But I take pride in knowing in my heart I am good. When I married, I took my husband's name as that was the way in our time. Hopefully, it will not always be the way but I always will be a Strong woman. When my Constance was born, it was the happiest moment of my life.

Born in 1675: Constance

Talents: **super breath**

Accomplishments: Used breath to put out fire

Words to Those Who Follow: **Love your parents...**

Thoughts: I am forever grateful that my mother was here to help me understand my powers. I cannot imagine what life must have been like for her growing up without having somebody to mentor and teach her. My father is also an amazing man, not many blacksmiths would readily accept having a woman that is far stronger than they are. I only hope my husband will be as understanding. Sadly, my husband, while being a good man would never understand a woman who is stronger than he. Yet I must marry so I can have a child as I wish to be a mother.

Born in 1694: Joan

Talents: **see-through vision**

Accomplishments: Worked with healing herbs

Words to Those Who Follow: **We must live on...**

Thoughts: These powers of mine... I'm never sure if they are a curse or a blessing. I can see into people... I can see-through walls... I fear I may be a demon sometimes. But then I find a person under a heavy tree branch and I save them and I understand these powers can bring good into the world. My husband is a doctor and a good man. He is fascinated by my abilities. That's what he calls them not powers. He tells me I can help people. I believe he is right. It is the turn of the century. Such an amazing time for my daughter to be born. My heart is broken... my dear husband has passed away, taken by the sickness that has taken so many others. My daughter, Desire, and I seem unaffected. That means we can help the sick without fear. I guess that is good. We must witness so much sadness. Our powers are a blessing and a curse.

Born in 1713: Desire

Talents: **Moving objects with thought...**

Accomplishments: Worked as a nurse

Words to Those Who Follow: **Passion and compassion**

go hand in hand...

     Thoughts: I decided I could best help the world as a nurse. I wish I could be a doctor but this world is not ready for a female doctor. If this world knew what I can do, they would be terrified of me. I am blessed with my mother's see-through vision. That, along with my other ability, is a great tool in aiding the wounded and sick. My voice also seems to bring comfort to people. I'm gladdened by that.

Born in 1732: Mary

     Talents: **Acid breath**

     Accomplishments: Studied the law on her own

     Words to Those Who Follow: **Without Law, there is chaos...**

     Thoughts: My mother and Grandmother have been such a wondrous help to me. Without their guidance, I do not know where I would be today. I decide to help defend the poor and the defenseless as they are the ones who need me most. But since I cannot display my abilities in public, I use the rules of law to defend them. I love the law, it is fair to all. I cannot call myself a lawyer but I am happy in the knowledge that I grasp the law as well as any man. Oh, the acid burps are such a nuisance. Hopefully, none of my daughters will get those.

Born in 1751: Rose

     Talents: **Super leap**

     Accomplishments: Freedom Fighter

Words to Those Who Follow: **Freedom is everything...**

Thoughts: What an exciting time as our country fights for independence from the Brits. I must fight as male and in disguise, but the expressions on the redcoats' faces when I bend their weapons is priceless. I say boo and they run like little children. I am glad my daughter, Remember, will grow up in an independent country.

Born in 1770: Remember

Talents: **Super intelligent**

Accomplishments: Inventor

Words to Those Who Follow: **Your brain is as powerful as your brawn...**

Thoughts: I work with an amazing man named Franklin. He is a fantastic inventor and has a mind almost as sharp as mine. The great thing is, he takes my ideas seriously. Though I cannot receive public credit for my accomplishments, Ben gives me much credit in private. He wishes he could tell the world about me. I tell him most of the world does not think like him. The day Ben passed from this Earth was one of the saddest of my life. I gladdened that he did get to meet my precious Sarah. I continue my work... I live for my Sarah and my work.

Born in 1789: Sarah

Talents: **Super breathing**

Accomplishments: Helped bring yoga to the United States

Words to Those Who Follow: **Grow your mind and body…**

Thoughts: Though we live in a new century, I do not find it much different from the old. Great Grandmother Mary says she sees changes, changes for the better. But changes take time. Time is one thing my mother and I and all the other women in our line do have. We do have trains that take us from place to place. I know that is progress. Today I heard that man duplicated God and made lightning. Some think it is a foolish endeavor. I find it amazing. I have not yet turned this book over to my daughter as I am still a young woman. Yet I have bared the passing of two husbands. One, because of war, the other due to infection. Part of me longs to go fight the tyrant Napoleon. With my abilities, I know I could crush his army. Of course, I would expose myself to the world. Is that such a bad thing? Mother insists it is. The world is not ready for us. It may never be. Still, my daughter, Katherine needs me.

Born in 1808: Katherine

    Talents: **Heat Vision**

    Accomplishments: Taught meditation

    Words to Those Who Follow: **Think before you act…**

    Thoughts: I sadly take this book far too soon. My mother passed away saving people in a massive fire. While the fire did not burn her skin, her lungs still ran out of air to breathe. Grandmother says even we must breathe.

Born in 1827: Humility

    Talents: **Super fart**

    Accomplishments: Writer

Words to Those Who Follow: **Words have power...**

Thoughts: My mother gave me this book and told me she hopes I will do more with our gifts than she did. I told my mother it is never too late to give to the world. Mother smiled. She told me she was a thinker, not a doer. I am including something called a photograph of mother and myself. These are truly amazing times.

I read the book, Frankenstein, today. I read the entire manuscript in one sitting. Funny, I felt sorry for the monster. Reading that story has caused me to want to share my words and views with the world. I am glad many find my stories of interest and amusement. Oh, beans and super strength are not a good mix!

Born in 1846: Becky

Talents: **Super charm**

Accomplishments: Artist

Words to Those Who Follow: **Look for the best in people while preparing for the worst...**

Thoughts: I joked with my mother about joining the Naval Academy. I do love the water. I could certainly outdo any of the males there. My mother told me that would not be wise. I married a naval officer instead. He is a good man, a kind man. Though I am not sure he would ever accept my abilities. A large log fell onto my husband's leg today. I removed it with ease. He passed away knowing the real me. He told me he wished I had shared my gifts with him sooner. Men, they can surprise you. My art helps me cope.

Born in 1865: Damarus

*Talents: **Super sight***

Accomplishments: War hero

*Words to Those Who Follow: **Even we have limits...***

Thoughts: Funny, how I take over this book at such an amazing yet hectic time. A great war has ended. I did my part fighting in disguise as a man like others of my kind before me have also done. I only wish I could have been by the president's side when he went to the theater. I could have saved him. I know I could have. I have done my share of fighting, now I will be the woman the world expects. I will marry and bear a child.

Born in 1884: Carol

*Talents: **Most power super fart***

Accomplishments: Saved town from stampeding herd with
fart

*Words to Those Who Follow: **Be calm...***

Thoughts: I love living in the 1900s, such an amazing time. Yes, I know future generations reading, this will look back at me and laugh, but we have subways, we have machines that clean our floors. We even have flying machines! I am reluctant to use my abilities. I do not wish to stand out. Oh in 1908, I made a visit to Siberia. After eating much raw cabbage I got a case of the winds... The destruction I caused was epic. I am glad I was camping alone at the time, but it showed me what my powers could do.

Born in 1903: Bella

*Talents: **Super-fast hands***

Accomplishments: Sports star

Words to Those Who Follow: **Be kind...**

Thoughts: Sadly, I never knew my mother. My grandmother told me she was a quiet but amazing fun loving woman. Apparently, my mother never liked to show her abilities, yet she died saving others in a massive fire. Reading this book, I see another of our line also passed this way. As powerful as we are, we still need to breathe. I'm still not sure how fast I can run but I know I can run much faster than automobiles. Grandmother and I went to something called a movie today. I told her soon the world would be ready for us. She just smiled at me. I chose to be a cook in a soup kitchen. There I cannot only feed people but I can learn of their problems and perhaps help them with my abilities. This world at war is terrible. Even I feel powerless to stop it.

Born in 1935: Ann

Talents: **Voice of calm**

Accomplishments: Professor

Words to Those Who Follow: **Never give up!**

Thoughts: The world fights another war to end all wars as my mother hands this book to me. I tell Mother that together we can fight the Nazis. We have the power! Mother convinced me the best way to fight is to be educated. I became a college professor. Today I read the comic, Superman. Perhaps, soon the world will be ready for a real super woman!

Born in 1950: Ellen

Talents: **Figured out scent could control people**

Accomplishments: Kept the Strong name
Words to Those Who Follow: **Women hold the true power...**

Thoughts: I decided to change my last name back to my ancestor's name of Strong. After all, it was the time of women's liberation. What better way to honor that concept than to be a Strong woman both literally and figuratively.

Born in 1968: Elizabeth (Beth)

Talents: **Worked on perfecting many powers**

Accomplishments: first to get a divorce – but stayed friends.

Words to Those Who Follow: **You can change people's minds at times...**

Thoughts: While I am grateful to all the Strong women who came before me, I am more grateful for being a powerful woman in the 80s. Finally, we can move up the corporate ladder to success. Using my strength and my abilities to influence people has allowed me much influence. I find influence works better than raw strength. It is more lasting and far reaching. I'm using my PR company to make the world a better place.

Born in 1985: Isabelle

Talents: **Great science talent**

Accomplishments: First medical doctor and PH.D.

Words to Those Who Follow: **Science is discovering, and** *knowledge is power...*

    Thoughts: My daughter, I am more of a woman of action than words. I am giving you this book early because I can sense greatness in you. I chose to use my powers in a subtle way, to heal. I am the first of the Strong women to become a medical doctor. My gifts have been a great aid to me in my profession. Your path may be very different to mine. The world is becoming a more accepting place. Who knows? Maybe they will be ready for a real super hero! If so, I can't think of a greater hero than you. I know I will be proud of you, whatever direction you choose. I am glad our genes mean I will be around for a long time to see you blossom.

Born in 2002: Lia

    Story to be told...

Thank you for reading Diary of a Super Girl: Book 1.

If you could leave a review, we would be very grateful.
Thank you so much!!!!!
John and Katrina

Some more books you may like:

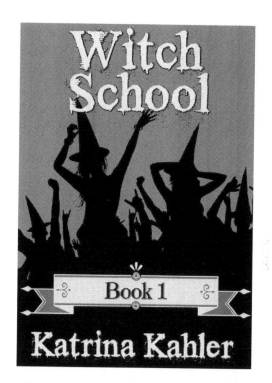

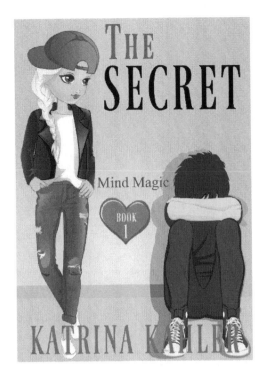

***

About the Authors

John Zakour *is a Humor/SF/Fantasy writer with a Master's Degree in Human Behavior. He has written thousands of gags for syndicated comics, comedians and TV Shows (including the Simpsons, Rugrats and Joan River's old TV show). John also writes a daily comic called Working Daze.*

Katrina Kahler *is the Best Selling Author of several series of books, including Julia Jones' Diary, Mind Reader, The Secret, Diary of a Horse Mad Girl, Twins, Angel, Slave to a Vampire and numerous Learn to Read Books for young children.*
Katrina lives in beautiful Noosa on the Australian coastline.

54088370R00068

Made in the USA
Middletown, DE
02 December 2017